VENGEANCE OF A QUEEN

The Resurrection of Queens, Book 2

ELIZABETH BROWN

Edited by Elemental Editing & Proofreading

Chapter Art by Jeanne Bradley

Cover by Fantastical Ink.

❀ Created with Vellum

Acknowledgments

This book is for Olivia. Woman, I do not have the words to express how fierce, savage, strong, and wonderful you are. You've inspired me in ways that I will never be able to thank you for. I want you know how just how much your friendship means to me. I wouldn't be here if it wasn't for you.

To my beta readers and critique partners, thank you so, so much for helping me get through this. This book was *not* easy to write. But your love and faith kept me going and helped me power through. I owe you.

To all my readers, gods...you guys are seriously the shit. I hope you all know that. And I hope that you all know just how much you all mean to me. Thank you for supporting me — a small time indie author. I was terrified when I released Discovery of a Queen, but y'all have just showered me with love. All of my books are for you. Love you!

This is a reminder to people who know me in real life... there's a bunch of SEX in this book. If that will make you uncomfortable, don't read it. I don't need weird looks at family dinners because y'all didn't realize I write smut with plot (professional smut if you will). I do. I'm not ashamed. Don't make this weird.

Three Fates pure to keep the gate,
past, present, future.
Should one Fate fall the seals will break,
maiden, mother, crone.
Two Fates more shall fall, and Hell shall wake,
life, death, rebirth.
New queens will rise to fight for light,
female, queen, goddess.
A sacrifice will heal the breach,
shifter, witch, vampire.
Three new Fates will be the key.

Prologue

I pace the confines of my cell. I'm infuriated that the Óir has the balls to change the game. Extinction level events happen, and they need to just accept that humanity's time is *over*. Their reign as "gods" is over.

I'm further enraged that Malick has continued to resist my control. Without Katia there to act as my conduit, I'll need to find a replacement to ensure his loyalty. I had to bring the witch under my wing and into Malick's life when he became despondent over needing to force changes in females to procure a child. Malick wouldn't take a woman unless she was willing—a fucking archdemon with a sense of honor, disgusting—so I made them willing. I reached out with my powers and instructed Katia on how to produce the serum, and once he injected them with the potion, I could control their minds.

All except for Lilith and the queen.

My rage almost blinds me at the thought of those two females. I thought it a fitting end to Morningstar's little pet to have her turned into my mindless puppet, but she repelled my influence, as did the queen. I know the Óir have some-thing to do with the queen's ability to resist my calling. I had my claws in her, bringing her ever closer to the edge, when suddenly, her life had faded away. I knew then that the Óir, despite their continued commitment to "not interfere" with "free will," had, in fact, interfered.

I pace faster as my fury continues to build.

The battle with the queen has caused Malick to question his commitment even further, despite knowing there are two additional queens he can take. I have yet to inform him of the newly turned queen, still not quite believing it myself. The only thing that keeps his interest is his attraction to the first queen. He felt a pull to her when he first saw her, but I needed to feed that spark. The amount of interference I've had to run lately has drained me. It's not easy to reach beyond the gates with my power. It's far easier for someone to send energy *in* than it is to send energy *out* of the pit, but I've honed my skills over the last several thousand years.

I ponder who to send to Malick now, never halting my strides across my confines. I can't send him my spy, who hides within the queen's ranks. That individual has proven far too valuable. I'm tempted to terminate Malick altogether. I have another archdemon who has proven far more loyal and malleable, though waking him will be difficult.

A nudge on my mind has me skidding to a halt.

Brother? a sweetly, seductive female tone trills in my mind. Surprise flairs through me. I haven't heard Lust's voice in millennia. *Satan? Is that you?* I haven't heard my true name in so long it takes me a moment to register she's used it.

Aye, Azazel. A wicked grin spreads across my face. If I can connect with my siblings, then I can change the damn game too, because it means the first seal has been broken.

Does this mean we're finally getting out of this horrid place?

Pride, Ramiel, sounds disgusted that he's had to remain in the pit for so long. I can't say I blame him.

You're not about to leave me out, Dagan growls.

My siblings, my brothers. I'm surprised Azazel is currently female, since he typically enjoys his male form. If he hasn't been able to spread his influence out of the pit, this must be how he's entertained himself. Abaddon and Beelzebub are the only two I haven't heard from, but I know it won't be long until they reach out to me just as the others have.

I had originally wanted to go about this alone, but the touch of my brothers' minds against mine reminds me that we are far more powerful together. I'll need them to take down the Óir and their queens.

And so I start to fill my siblings in on my plan.

~

Malick

IT'S BEEN weeks since the battle with the little queen and her community. *Weeks.* When I awakened in that cave, I assumed that mere moments had passed. That prick, Wrath, had kept me suspended for bloody weeks.

While I can accept that it was in my best interest, as I'd desperately needed to heal, the thought of losing so much time infuriates me, especially now that I know of Ayla's sisters. Wrath had a point about letting her do all the work, but it's not that simple. I need to find a new bloody mage since the little queen went and killed mine. I also need to assess the losses to my ranks and ensure that my facilities are still intact. I understand the Sin is in Hell, but using a touch of critical thinking wouldn't kill him.

I'm back at the house I held Ayla in, picking through

what's left of the place and trying to determine my next step. Is it even worth it to continue down this path? While ruling beside Morningstar would be spectacular, I've been at this for centuries now, and frankly, I've grown tired. Exhausted, really.

Now that I'm truly thinking about it, my heart hasn't been in this venture, not really, since well before I captured Aine. Why had I continued?

A cloaked figure appears beside me. I don't sense any threat, so I merely observe. They sought me out, so there's no need for me to engage in conversation unless they do.

"Lord Malick." I can't determine if they are male or female, which tells me they are using a spell to disguise their voice. My eyes narrow in suspicion. "Lord Wrath has sent me to aid you in your quest against the queens."

Interesting phrasing, "against the queens." I'm not specifically against them. It's quite the opposite—I want to mate with one to produce the Antichrist. While that may not align with Ayla's goals, I certainly have no wish to kill her.

That realization startles me. I have no intention of murdering any of the queens. My main objective is to obtain a mate. This rocks me to my core.

"And who, exactly, are you?" I'll play along for now. After all, Ayla has officially mated with the male dragon, so my best hope of mating with a queen rests with her sisters.

"My identity is of no concern. What matters is that I can lend you the magical assistance you need for success." My suspicion increases. "Lord Wrath has a plan."

"Does he now?" Suddenly, I'm filled with renewed dedication to the cause. Part of my mind rebels against this wave of excitement. Wasn't I just saying I was tired of all this? I can feel something slither into my mind, burrowing deep.

"He does." The voice sounds pleased. "And he's delighted that you continue to dedicate yourself to the cause."

That flare of rebellion is back, only to be pushed aside by whatever has burrowed into my mind. I frantically attempt to hold onto that feeling of mutiny, not wanting to lose myself in these false thoughts. It's no use, however, because my own thoughts slip through my grasp like sand.

Chapter One

Ten Weeks Ago.

When the light from Ayla's attack fades, my heart hammers loudly in my chest as I pant slightly. Fuck me. She's killed all of the lower-level demons. That's badass. But something else catches my attention—Malick. Or the lack thereof. He's not in the ground anymore.

Where the hell did that fucker go? I glance around and notice everyone from our community is doing the same. Shit. No one seems to have any idea what the hell transpired.

Those of you who saw what happened, I want to be debriefed as soon as we're safely back at the community, is that clear? Caleb booms through our bonds. He must be using his mate bond with Ayla to talk to all of us. Immediately, the witches still able to do so begin creating portals back to our community land.

Strong hands grip the tops of my arms, spinning me around to face one of the most handsome men I've ever met.

Malcolm.

My panther purrs inside my head. She seems to like the witch just as much as I do. His scent, which reminds me of fresh rain in the desert, has been driving me insane since he showed up at our doorstep with the rest of the Council. Surprisingly, his hair is pulled back from his face today. He usually prefers to keep it loose and flowing around his shoulders.

I don't get the chance to think anymore. Malcolm's mouth lands on mine and my brain shuts down. My eyes slide closed, and stars instantly burst behind my eyelids. Time seems to slow as my entire being becomes solely focused on the sensation of his lips against mine. My panther releases a low, pleased growl.

Mate. Holy hell. Talk about life changing days.

~

Four Weeks Ago.

AFTER EVERYTHING AYLA'S been through, I'm surprised she hasn't taken it easier on herself. The woman has been like a damn machine since she woke up a few days ago. And the only reason we aren't heading to Ireland right now is because she wants to take some time out to train me.

I'm a damn queen. It's been six weeks, but awe still fills me every time I think about it.

My mind flashes back to the moment on the battlefield when I inadvertently exploded a demon by turning him inside out. My stomach still gets a bit queasy just thinking about it. I'd been feeling off all day, amped for the battle ahead in a way I'd never felt before. I love a good brawl, but this was completely different. I wouldn't go so far as to say blood-thirsty, but I was certainly eager to get into the thick of things and rip demons apart with my touch.

Accompanying those images is a memory I've tried my best to shove into a little box in my mind and forget. After Ayla released her life mojo on all the demons and the dust had settled enough for all of us to determine that we were all alive and going to stay that way, I felt Malcolm grab my arms. I stared up at him with excitement buzzing through my veins as he leaned in and kissed the ever loving daylights out of me. It wasn't a sweet, gentle first kiss. It was a kiss to lay claim to my very soul. A kiss that curled my toes, blew my damn head off, and melted my knees.

And it hadn't happened again since.

My panther lets out a low rumble of annoyance at the thought. We finally found our mate, he planted the mother of all kisses on me, and then ignored me? Not all shifters are able to determine their mates by first scent, and there isn't always that instant flash of heat the way Ayla describes what happened with her and Caleb. For some of us, it can take a while for us to realize what's directly in front of our damn faces—especially if our mate isn't another shifter.

I'm not sure if becoming a queen made me realize Malcolm is my mate sooner, or if I'd have known the instant his lips landed on mine anyway. That doesn't matter. What matters is that the man has been avoiding touching me ever since. He's been shooting me hungry looks, but he hasn't acted on them. I've been so busy trying to get my new magic under control that by the time I think about acting on the mating instinct, he's already scuttled away somewhere.

~

Present

As I step through the portal to Ireland with Malcolm beside me, I swear to all that is good in this world that if he doesn't touch me soon, I am going to rip his head off. You can't go around kissing people like that once and then never touch them again. Is he brain damaged?

He's a witch, Olivia. My panther gently brushes against my mind. *He doesn't feel the urge to mate the way we do.* Goddess, how can he not feel this heat? It's eating me alive. While I'm a dominant shifter female, I have no desire to go after a man who doesn't want me, even if he is my mate. No. If he wants me, he needs to step right the fuck up and say so.

What if we nudge him along? My panther has no problem with the idea of us rubbing all over him. *We don't need to go at him like a cat in heat, but just give him enough of an indication that you're interested. We don't know how witches mate. What if it's not instinctual?*

I suppose she has a point. I refuse to throw myself at a man, but there's no harm in subtly nudging said man, right?

I've been so caught up in my thoughts that I haven't noticed the stunning scenery around me. Now that it's claimed my attention, my breath catches and my eyes go wide. I've never been to Ireland before, but I've seen pictures. Pictures do not do the beauty of this land justice. The thrum of power, ancient and wise, pulses out of the very ground here.

Ayla said we'd be coming out of the portals at the Cliffs of Moher, where her village used to be. The crashing of the sea against the cliffs only serves to amplify the power here. I can feel it singing through every nerve, every cell. I want to dance and cry out in joy. The energy is just so pure and light. I let it roll over me.

Ayla stands in front of me, slowly spinning with her arms out by her sides. She has an expression I'm sure is mirrored on my face. Wonder. Joy. Power. Her connection to this place is stronger than mine, so I can only imagine how she's feeling.

"I hate to break up the love fest," Caleb calls, startling both Ayla and me out of our commune with nature, "but we need to find somewhere to stay. We can't be out in the open."

"I agree." Malcolm moves to stand next to me, gently placing a hand on the small of my back, causing my panther to purr.

"Our cottage was right on the cliffs." Ayla sounds wistful, her eyes unfocused. "Ma used to take us out flying at night over the water."

As she speaks, I feel a surge of magic drawing me closer to the cliff's edge. Following the pull of the magic, I inch closer to the drop-off until I feel a large, warm hand close over my shoulder.

"What the hell are you doing, Liv?" Malcolm growls. "Get away from that damn cliff."

"Don't you feel it?" I can still feel the pull of the magic, so I let my own magic respond. It flares out around me, the beautiful amethyst mist shimmering in the light. It shines around a dome that appears to be empty, until it flashes and reveals a small cottage where nothing had been before.

Ayla gasps. "The cottage!" She doesn't make a move to get any closer, and Caleb comes up to wrap his arms around her.

"How did you know that was there?" Malcolm questions, still firmly gripping my arm.

"You didn't feel that?" I ask, looking at the others around us. Everyone shakes their heads, staring at me oddly. "There was this pull, I couldn't ignore it."

"She almost went off the damn cliff," Malcolm snarls. "The magic almost killed her. And listen to her! She sounds like a damn zombie!"

I bristle at his words. "Excuse the fuck out of you. I do not sound like a zombie. It's not my fault your 'wand' couldn't find magic even if magic hit it upside the head!" My rebuke ends on a shout. While I intended to be subtle about my approach to Malcolm, he just pissed me off, so I needed to, rightfully, call his manhood into question.

Girl, you have so much explaining to do. Ayla's laughter echoes through our bond, and I grin in response. Malcolm starts to turn an interesting shade of purple, his mouth opening and closing as he struggles to respond. *You just insulted a man's penis. That's savage. Something has absolutely gone down between the two of you and you will tell me.* Ayla proceeds to laugh out loud, causing Malcolm to turn and glower at her. Caleb has the good sense to hide his face by burying it in Ayla's hair, but there's no mistaking the shaking of his shoulders.

"My wand," Malcolm starts, pulling me flush against him, "can find magic perfectly fine."

"Prove it." The two worst words to ever be spoken between two individuals who have sexual tension so thick it would take a chainsaw to cut through it. Malcolm tenses against me, his eyes narrowing on my parted lips. I decide to push him just a bit more by slowly sliding my tongue along my bottom lip. His eyes narrow further, and a low growl forces its way out of his chest. It's impressive since he isn't a shifter.

And then his mouth is on mine, our lips fusing together as his hand tangles in my hair tightly, moving my head exactly where he wants it. I groan, and Malcolm uses that moment to plunge his tongue into my mouth. There is nothing gentle about this kiss. It's not the kiss of two mates discovering one another. It's the kind of kiss that tells you a man wants all of you, no holding back.

My mind stalls for a minute, unsure. Malcolm is my mate, and the urge to climb him like a tree is so damn strong. The fact that he hasn't touched me in weeks makes me feel insecure, but his kiss quickly wipes the feeling away. I'm only just starting to settle into the kiss when I hear a loud cough behind us.

"Guys?" Ayla is amused, and I can tell she's struggling not to laugh. "I appreciate the show. Malcolm, I need to give you a solid nine for hand placement, passion, and enthusiasm, but a one on timing."

Caleb chuckles.

I pull away from Malcolm, blinking several times to try to get my brain to work properly again. Malcolm's grip in my hair tightens, not letting me pull too far away. He brings his lips close to my ear and whispers, "This isn't finished."

Damn it. I don't think I packed enough panties to be talked to like that. My panther purrs so aggressively it makes my chest vibrate. Malcolm's eyes go wide and drop to my chest as I continue to purr, a wicked grin spreading across his lips.

Caleb slaps his hand on Malcolm's back, breaking the moment. Malcolm throws me one last heated look before walking off with the alpha, going to make sure that the cottage is safe enough for us to investigate. Ayla is suddenly by my side, a shit-eating grin plastered on her face.

"You told me it was nothing. That you'd just been training with him." She waggles her eyebrows at me. "Is that what the kids are calling hot, nasty, sweaty sex?"

A surprised laugh bursts from my lips. "No, that's not what the kids are calling any form of sex." I shake my head. "He kissed me on the battlefield that day with Malick. Just laid the mother of all kisses on me and then nothing. Literally nothing. For weeks! And now he just swoops in with that?" I groan and tug slightly on my hair. "What the fuck was that? What am I supposed to even do with that?" I glance over at my friend to see her fighting back more laughter.

"Oh, honey." She sobers upon seeing the frustration on my face. "He's a dumb male, but learn from my experience with Caleb—don't hold back and go after what you want. I can feel the mate bond forming inside you, Olivia. I know what he is. Witches are different, they don't have the pull the same way we do, but his magic will draw him to you, even if he doesn't realize why. If you don't want to give it time, I can help with Operation Cave Explorer."

"I'm sorry" —I can't keep my laughter contained— "Operation Cave Explorer?" Ayla lifts one of her hands so it forms an O-shape and inserts the forefinger of her other hand, rather aggressively, in and out of the ring several times, winking lewdly at me. "Why the fuck am I even friends with you?"

"You love me, and you know it." She beams at me. "Now let's go see what those idiots are up to. We can form a solid plan to have your cave explored later."

I groan but allow her to lead me toward the cottage. The men have gone inside, so presumably it's safe for us to do so as well. I crack open the door and allow Ayla to go in ahead of me. It's her family home, after all. Despite her earlier reaction to seeing the cottage, she's more composed now, her eyes wide as though she's trying to take everything in all at once.

The cottage has been extremely well preserved. I wouldn't have assumed it had been sitting here empty for over four hundred years. As soon as I follow Ayla through the doorway, the door slams shut, the snick of the lock engaging causing all four of us to freeze. A gentle rumble shakes the cottage, slowly getting louder and more aggressive with the passing minutes. My hand just slaps onto the door before the cottage is plunged into darkness.

Chapter Two

The silence that follows is almost deafening. I find it disconcerting not being able to see or hear anyone. I can feel them all through my bonds, however, and while there's a lot of shock going around, everybody seems to be fine.

"Everyone okay?" Caleb's voice booms through the darkness. Ayla murmurs that she's fine, followed by Malcolm's affirmation that he's okay.

"Yeah. I'm good. What about everyone we left outside? What the hell just happened?" The darkness around me is so thick it seems to swallow my words, and for a moment, I'm afraid the others can't hear me. Malcolm brushes his fingers against mine, quickly taking hold of my hand, and I squeeze his fingers. I'm surprised at how reassuring his touch is.

We're in the darkness for a moment longer before harsh light floods the room. My pupils contract painfully at the sudden attack. I'm disoriented for a moment as I take in the small cottage.

We're standing on a packed dirt floor, and there's a large fireplace that takes up the wall to the right. There are three beds tucked into the corner, and a handcrafted wooden table in the middle of the room. A door directly across from the main entrance leads into another room—I assume it's where Ayla's parents slept. It's cozy and fits with how people lived five hundred years ago.

When my gaze falls on Ayla again, she's staring intently at the fireplace mantel. Malcolm and Caleb open the door to assure themselves everything is fine, and then they speak to the people we left outside.

"It must have just been whatever security spell was placed on the cottage." Malcolm's voice drifts over to me, but I'm not really paying attention to the men. Ayla won't take her gaze away from the fireplace.

I move to stand next to her, turning my gaze in the same direction. Carved into the mantle is an intricate design of the waxing, full, and waning moons with a representation of the goddesses through the full moon. It's all done in delicate Celtic knotwork. I kind of want to touch it. The scene from *Finding Nemo*, where Dory wants to touch the baby jellyfish, comes to mind, so I keep my hands to myself.

Ayla doesn't seem to have the same hesitation I do. She steps closer to the mantel, gingerly running her fingers along the carving. It glows softly and I step forward, reaching out to touch the figure as if my hand has a mind of its own. There's a thrum of power in the air as the space between my finger and the mantle dwindles.

I finally make contact, and a strong bolt of magic flairs around us. My gasp is caught in my throat as the world goes dark. *Mierda*.

~

IN THE NEXT HEARTBEAT, we are standing in the middle of a vicious battle. My hand is already closed around the necklace

Kelly gave us, and both her and Darcy shimmer into being beside us. Screams rend the air and the scent of blood clogs my nose. I stiffen, ready to defend myself, but Ayla puts a hand on my arm before I can act.

"Do you recognize anyone?" I ask her. Since the magical Celtic knot was in her old cottage, it's safe to assume that even though I'm along for this magical ride, I've got no horse in the race. I look over at Kelly and Darcy. I can see their mouths moving, but I can't hear them. Odd. It seems like they can hear us though.

"No."

That's odd. Why would the magical design show us something that isn't related to Ayla? I'm scanning the battle when I catch sight of someone familiar. "Look!" I point. "Brigid!"

I haven't had the chance to meet the goddess in person, but everyone knows what Brigid looks like. We all know what all of the gods and goddesses look like. Brigid is clashing swords with a tall male, and the visual differences between them are startling.

Dios Mío.

The male is well over seven feet tall with skin so dark it seems to absorb the light around him, and his eyes are gold with blood-red irises. He's got horns, similar to an archdemon's, that wrap around his skull and end in lethally sharp points by his chin. His stark white hair is shorn close on the sides and braided into intricate knots on the top of his head, the color providing a staggering contrast against his skin.

Brigid, on the other hand, seems to emit light. Her skin is so pale and fair that I can clearly see her golden veins, even from a distance. Her fiery red hair is braided down her back with beads. Unlike most depictions of her, her eyes are currently gold as well, but with bright blue irises.

The two trade blows that ring above the battle raging around them, both completely focused on the other. I'm so engrossed in their fierce fight that for several moments, I don't notice Ayla gently tapping my arm.

"Liv..." Ayla's voice is quiet, shocked. "Focus on the battle. There are only seven of the dark ones. The gods and goddesses are teaming up to battle *seven*."

That snaps me out of my intense focus. I quickly glance around and realize she's right. There are only seven dark beings, all surrounded by multiple gods and goddesses, save for the solo fight between Brigid and her dark entity. Ice drips down my spine as my eyes continue to bounce between the seven dark creatures and the divine surrounding them. These seven creatures can hold off a small army of gods and goddesses.

Santa Mierda. What the hell are they?

Dread makes my stomach churn as the scene continues to unfold. My attention returns to Brigid, and I notice she's struggling more than she was a few minutes ago. What on earth are we watching?

The scene fades and is replaced with a large hall, with the gods and goddesses sitting around a long rectangular table. They are bickering, and I can't make out any of what they are discussing.

Odin stands, slamming his fists against the table. "Enough!" His voice rings around the room, causing everyone at the table to fall silent. "We all know what has to be done. We need to banish the Härja. We have to pool our powers and create a prison strong enough to hold them."

"But that will require a sacrifice." Isis stands, her expression livid as she glares at Odin. "Not only would one of our guardians have to sacrifice themselves in an abhorrent manner, but one of our own would also need to be banished to this prison."

"I'm well aware of what is at stake. There is no other choice," Odin argues.

"I will go." A quiet voice causes all heads to turn in its direction. A stunningly handsome man with bright white wings stands. "I will anchor the prison."

"Lucifer," Isis starts, but a shake of his head silences her.

"Odin is right. This is the only option. It will take our guardians many years to banish the Härja to the pit. It will be ready for them. I will see to it."

"Then it is done."

The world once again goes black.

Now, the four of us stand beside a woman who looks a lot like Ayla. She's kneeling before an altar dedicated to Brigid, her head bowed.

"Mum," Ayla murmurs, the Irish accent I know she's worked hard to get rid of coming back full force. She raises her hand as if to touch her mother but stays rooted to her spot.

"Please." Her mother's voice is thick with tears. "Please, do not make my babes go through such trials."

A shimmering female figure steps up beside the altar— Brigid. The only thing that has changed about her appearance since the last vision is her hair, which is now loose about her shoulders.

"Aine," Brigid begins, her tone musical, "I do not wish to cause you harm, daughter." She kneels beside Aine, taking Aine's hands in hers. "But your daughters are Fates. They are a necessary part of the balance we have strived so hard to maintain."

"I do not mean ye any disrespect, milady" —Aine bows her head—"but I cannot allow my children to go through such horrors. I have heard the prophecy. They are but babes. To have such responsibility thrust upon them..."

"And that is why we shall do all we can to keep them safe."

"But what of the prophecy? There is no way they can truly be safe."

"We know not its origin, but we have put fail-safes in place to ensure they will not fight alone." Brigid sets her hand on Aine's cheek, gently tilting the other woman's face up. "We are blessing three new Fates who will fight alongside your daughters."

The scene once again changes, but Ayla and I are frozen in place before the hearth. Now, Aine and a man I assume is Ayla's father are huddled by the door of the cottage. The night is brightly lit by both the full moon and the Milky Way galaxy shining overhead.

"My love," Ayla's father rumbles, "do not fret. We have been given guidance. Our daughters will be safe until their time comes." He tenderly presses his forehead to Aine's, and my heart squeezes at the intimate display.

"Cillian. We are merely buying them time. The war that is to come—"

"Is theirs to fight."

A sob pierces the still night, and my heart breaks as I watch them discuss the fate of their beloved children. Ayla knew nothing about any of this until recently. My gaze flicks to her, and the longing evident on her face causes tears to sting the backs of my eyes. I reach out and take her hand, squeezing it gently. She doesn't take her gaze away from her parents, but her fingers curl against mine, clutching them as though they are her only lifeline.

"We will hide one in the new world, one in the old world, and one where life began." Aine's voice is stronger, and determination illuminates her eyes as she pulls back from Cillian and meets his gaze. "I will not make them vulnerable by keeping them together."

"It's a good plan, love. How will they wake?"

The world goes dark again before we're able to hear her answer. *Mierda*.

MALCOLM GRIPS my shoulders as I'm flung out of the vision. My breaths are coming out in soft pants as my eyes roam his face. He's worried about me. Everything about his body language screams it at me. My heart stutters before pounding loudly in my chest. I'm surprised he can't hear the damn thing.

"What the hell happened to you two?" Caleb's voice rips my gaze from Malcolm's face. I glance over to see him cradling Ayla's cheeks in his hands, his eyes frantically examining her.

"We..." Ayla pauses. "Saw my mother. The symbol on the mantel..." She glances over at it, causing the rest of us to look over as well. "It showed us things."

"And you were pulled into this vision too?" Malcolm questions, drawing my attention back to him.

"Yeah. The magic called to me." I shake my head. "I'm not sure why, but I couldn't have fought it even if I wanted to. Everything about the magic just felt right."

"I didn't feel the magic," Ayla interjects. "There was just a sense of home."

"This is the second time you've felt magic like this." Malcolm's brow creases with concern. "I'm worried you're pushing your new powers too fast."

"What?" I look at him, confused. How does my ability to feel magic relate to overusing my powers? "Witches have different abilities. It stands to reason that different queens will have different abilities also." I take a step back from him, giving him a look that clearly says I think he's slightly brain damaged. "Ayla can read auras, and while I get hints of them, more so from demons and people who have been tainted, I can feel magic. It has nothing to do with how I've been using my new powers."

"How can you be so sure?" Malcolm challenges as he starts pacing, running his hand through his hair and fiddling with his large framed glasses. "You've only had your powers for a short time. You haven't mentioned feeling magic like this before."

"Because we haven't dealt with anything as strong or ancient before."

Hun. Ayla nudges at my bond. *He's worried about you. Take it from me, being rational with him isn't going to work right now.*

Aren't men the ones who always claim women are irrational when they're upset or worried?

Hypocrites, the lot of them. Doesn't change the fact that he's had his feathers ruffled.

He's a big boy...

Who needs a hug.

Mierda. She's probably right. Malcolm is my mate, and every instinct inside me is screaming for me to comfort him. He's concerned about my wellbeing, which is touching and sweet, but beneath that it feels as though he doesn't genuinely think I am coping with everything that's been thrown my way lately...or maybe it's that I'm not coping the way he wants me to.

I know the man has faith in me. He wouldn't have offered to train me himself if he didn't think I could hold my own. I cock my head as I watch him pace and continue to rant. I know I've questioned his feelings lately, but that kiss outside the cottage and his actions now suggest he does have feelings for me—I think. Men are confusing as hell.

I mentally nudge Ayla to drag Caleb away for a minute, so Malcolm and I can be alone. He doesn't notice, still too caught up in his ramblings. It's kind of cute. He's gotten himself all worked up because he's worried about me. It's needless, but I haven't had anyone worry about me like this before, and despite the independent woman in me that wants to be offended, it's still sort of sweet. I watch him for another few seconds before placing myself directly in his path.

"Malcolm." He stops moving and ranting and just stares at me. "You've been training me for a while now." I gently take his hands. "I need you to trust me when I say I'm not overusing my powers. I promise I'm fine."

His shoulders sag increasingly the longer he stares at me. "Damn it, woman. I know you're fine." His hand whips out and snakes around the back of my neck, pulling me against his chest. "You're too important."

My heart slams to a stop and my body freezes against his. Too important? Does that mean...?

My thoughts scatter as Malcolm tips my chin up and molds his lips to mine.

Chapter Three

I remember feeling Ayla's emotions through the bond when she first found Caleb, the ones she didn't want to admit to, even to herself. I also remember thinking I wouldn't feel that way about my mate—all soft and girly with little hearts flying over my head, or like I needed to jump his bones right that minute or explode.

Dios Mío. I couldn't have been more wrong.

The need to feel his skin against mine rages through my body. The only thing stopping me is the knowledge that Ayla and Caleb, along with a hundred or so others, are right outside. But that doesn't stop me from sliding my hands up Malcolm's chest and into his hair. I've never really been one for long hair on men, but it's quickly becoming a weakness. I can see why men like long hair on women, because having something to hold on to is sexy as hell.

His fingers drop from my chin, and both hands land on my hips, pulling me flush against him as our tongues start dueling. We kiss as though we'll never be able to touch each other again, as though we're the only two people left on this earth—hell, in this galaxy. I know we don't have long before someone knocks on the cottage door, but I can't seem to drag myself away from him. He kissed me for the first time months ago and has kissed me twice in the last few hours. It's almost as if I'm afraid to let go of him and have him take months before he kisses me again.

I'd combust if that happened.

My panther is clawing at me, desperate to mark her mate and bask in the knowledge that this man is ours. She had been surprisingly quiet while Ayla and I had been on our little vision quest, but now...now she's all teeth and claws, screaming at me not to let him leave this room without first making it clear that he will never touch another female the way he's touching us now.

Malcolm nibbles on my lower lip, pulling me out of my battle with my panther as shivers race down my spine. Just as I'm about to retaliate and sink my teeth into his lip, he pulls away to lean his forehead against mine. I can feel his breath against my face as he pants quietly, and when I glance up, his eyes capture mine and hold me hostage.

"I'm trying to give you space." His voice is low and strained.

He's what?

Who the fuck said I wanted or needed space?

Does this mean we could have had him as our mate months ago? My panther sounds just as pissed as I feel. I'm getting ready to pimp slap him.

That's exactly what it sounds like, cabrón. My answer is a low growl. I'm sure someone else might have appreciated that he held himself back the last few months because of the transition, but it would have made everything easier if I had him with me. Yes, he's been training me, but he wasn't there during the long, lonely nights when I sat awake, trying to make heads or tails of what all of this meant for me. I didn't have anyone to talk to.

And he still wants to hold himself back, my panther seethes. I know I had just decided to take some initiative here, but how the hell do I get him to change his mind if he's determined to "give me space?" What a load of bullshit.

I pull back from him, moving far enough away so he isn't touching me and can't touch me again without crossing the room. If he wants to give me space, then I'll make sure there's a hell of a lot of space. My panther growls low inside me. We both know I'm being petty right now, but I'm hurt. I want to lash out, but know if I do so without thinking, I could ruin everything. Goddess, this whole mate thing is terrible. *No mames.*

I look over at Malcolm, who's now standing on the other end of the room appearing almost lost. My heart clenches, and I want to go to him, but his words still echo in my mind. The need to comfort wars with the need to punch him in the throat.

"I never said I wanted or needed space," I hiss, my words coming out sharper than I intended. Frankly, I'm surprised I said anything at all. "You made that assumption without consulting me." Okay, so we're planting the flag. Cool.

"You just found out you're a queen. Your powers have just been unlocked. I'm not about to add to that." He's got this stubborn expression on his face, and the urge to throat punch him grows. "You need to learn how to handle your powers, not get caught up in anything else."

"Like a hunt for a prophecy and other missing queens?" Two can play at this game. I cross my arms and cock out my hip. "Because I don't see how going on this little jaunt is training me in my new powers, but please, explain to the little woman who can't make decisions on her own."

Watching Malcolm turn an interesting shade of purple gives me a sick sense of pleasure. He knows I have him trapped, and while I don't like being "that girl," I'm also not about to have him treat me like a damn piece of china that needs to be kept on a shelf. If he's afraid of me, and he should be, that's on him. Let's not be placing blame anywhere else but squarely where it needs to be.

"You are not a little woman who can't make her own decisions," he says at last, "but you don't need the distraction right now."

"I don't need the distraction? Or *you* don't need the distraction?" I never realized my voice could hit this octave.

"I—" He's saved when Ayla opens the door and pokes her head into the room.

"As much as I'd love to give you two all the time in the world to do the nasty, we need to talk about what happened and what our game plan is." She looks between us, her eyes narrowing. "And don't think I'm not going to ask about this." She points at us. "There's a lot of space in there." Her head disappears and the door closes again.

I don't give Malcolm a chance to say anything as I head to the door. He needs to figure his shit out, and I'm not going to do it for him. I'm not going to go easy on him either. He wants to give me space, so I'm going to show him just how difficult that's going to be. He pissed me off and brought out my petty bitch, so we're about to go to war.

～

I'M STANDING NEXT to Ayla when Malcolm makes his way out of the cottage. He quickly moves to stand opposite me, unable to meet my eyes. *Pendejo*. I roll my eyes and return my focus to Ayla.

"So what did you see when you touched the mark on the mantel?" Caleb glances between us. "You just froze and wouldn't respond to anything. It was freaky as hell."

"At first we were observing a battle," I explain, "but things kept changing." Ayla nods. We launch into our description of what happened. Caleb and Malcolm remain silent but attentive the entire time.

"Seven dark creatures fighting against the gods..." Malcolm murmurs, lost in thought and once again playing with his glasses. "The gods then said they needed to banish them. What the hell does Härja mean?" He whips out his phone and starts typing. "Ravage. It's a Swedish word."

"Want to share what's going through your mind with the class?" Caleb's voice jars Malcolm out of his musings.

"There are a lot of different theologies and lore here. It's not that easy to make heads or tails of it all." Malcolm starts to pace. "Their eyes seemed similar?" We nod. "It's possible they are a similar species. Maybe different races. Then there's the fact that it took multiple deities to take on a single one of these Härja. And where did they banish them to?"

"And how does all of this play into the prophecy?" Ayla remarks. "The goddesses told me that Malick wasn't our main enemy. Is he in league with one of these Härja? This is also the second time I've been called a Fate, but I thought those were Greek goddesses, the ladies who cut the string of a mortal's life."

"I'm relaying all of this to Connor," Caleb informs us. "He and Kelly can do some research. It's good she was there to see some of this firsthand."

"Anyone else feel like we just jumped out of the frying pan and into the fire?" I look around. "Because it seems like we're pawns in a game where it's just our lives on the line. I'd kind of like some answers."

"Why couldn't Brigid say all of this when I saw her while I was held by Malick?" Ayla runs a hand through her hair. "We could see it, but she couldn't tell me about it? Why is all of this so convoluted?"

I throw my hands up. "Hell if I know!"

"This is so frustrating." Ayla looks ready to murder someone—not that I can blame her, I'd love to maul something also.

"Why don't we take a break and get ourselves set up in the manor?" Malcolm suggests, casting a look at me that I can't quite interpret. "I think we could all use some downtime before we hash this out. Besides, it'll take some time for Connor and Kelly to do research."

"You're right," I grumble with a glance at Ayla. "We're not going to be able to solve this here and now. Girls' night?"

Ayla grins broadly at me, thrilled with the idea. "Absolutely."

"Hey!" Caleb protests, but Ayla shoots him a death glare, and he glowers at her with his arms crossed over his chest. "Fine."

Malcolm opens a portal that only jumps us a few miles away. The manor is owned by the Council and is larger than the packhouse back home. While we could just portal home, this doesn't take as much effort for the caster and is easier on the rest of us, since jumping between time zones over and over again is a bitch. My mouth drops open when I get my first good look at the manor. It's a freaking castle! I'm about to sleep in an honest to goodness castle. My inner five-year-old is squealing with glee right now.

"You didn't tell me we were staying in a castle, asshole." I hear Ayla's punch land somewhere on Caleb, and I can't quite hide my cackle.

"You and Olivia are queens. It seemed appropriate."

Ayla grumbles at his response, and I have to fight to keep myself from grinning like an idiot.

My gaze once again finds Malcolm. He's watching me intently. My brow lifts as I hold his stare, but he only continues to watch me. Fuck it. Let him watch. I flip my hair over my shoulder and strut into the manor.

"Bedrooms are on the third floor," he states, not far behind me. "Caleb and Ayla are the first door on the right. Feel free to choose any of the others."

Without glancing back at him, I give him a thumbs-up and head upstairs. He wants to be a pain in my ass, okay. But I'm a motherfucking queen. He's going to learn that I'm the biggest royal pain in the ass ever.

~

LATER THAT NIGHT, Ayla and I created a blanket and pillow fort in one of the sitting rooms. We've got popcorn and witch wine, we're in our pajamas, and we are wasted. It's nice just to hang out with her, especially after everything we've been through. I've missed just sitting around her house or the packhouse with a glass of wine. It feels as though we haven't had any time to just be friends since she challenged Morgan. We need to decompress, reaffirm our friendship, and just have a night where we don't need to worry about being killed.

Ayla starts humming the first few bars of "Sweet but Psycho" by Ava Max, and since I've just emptied another bottle of witch wine into my cup, I decide to get into it and use the wine bottle as my mic. "Oh, she's sweet but a psycho! A little bit psycho!"

Ayla joins in with a giggle. "Grab a cop kinda crazy! She's poison but tasty!"

We dissolve into a fit of giggles before Ayla straightens. "Are you thinking what I'm thinking?"

"White girl wasted karaoke?"

"Yes!" Ayla screams out in joy. I hear two sets of footsteps outside of the sitting room, but we're happy in our little ladies only fort, so I don't bother to try to see who's watching our drunken shenanigans.

The mate bond, though, doesn't let me ignore the fact that Malcolm is one of the people poking their heads in to watch us, so I take out my phone and connect it to the Bluetooth speakers in the room to blast "Blow Your Mind (Mwah)" by Dua Lipa. Ayla and I stand, dancing and getting into the music. We get a verse in and hit the chorus when I turn to stare Malcolm dead in the eye as I sing.

If you don't like the way I talk, then why am I on your mind?
If you don't like the way I rock, then finish your glass of wine
We fight and we argue, you'll still love me blind
If we don't fuck this whole thing up
Guaranteed, I can blow your mind
Mwah!

I finish by blowing a kiss and shooting Malcolm a wink. This sends Ayla into hysterics, and she screams, "Savage!"

We collapse onto our pillows in a fit of giggles. Caleb comes in, chuckling softly, to tell us that ladies' night has come to an end. He picks up a still giggling Ayla and carries her out of the room. I'm still flopped on my mountain of pillows, giggling quietly to myself, when Malcolm appears over me. The look in his eyes instantly quiets my giggles as he leans down to scoop me up.

Shocked, I gape at him as he hauls me tightly against his chest, my arms wrapping quickly around his neck. The heat of his body seeps into me, causing my already slightly fuzzy head to become more muddled. I can't stop the purr that starts to vibrate my entire body as his scent envelops me. It's like he's a drug I can't get enough of.

"You're wrong," he says quietly. "You're the drug."

Shit. Did I say that out loud? I blink up at him, my mind occupied with trying to resist melting into him as my purr still reverberates in my chest.

Not out loud. His voice is a low rumble in my head, a caress I didn't know I wanted or needed until that moment. *The bond is already forming.*

My brain stalls out for a moment. The *mate* bond? I vaguely remember Ayla rage venting about the mate bond starting to form without her knowledge because it's what queens do...and I'm a queen now. Typically, shifters don't form the bond until they've fully accepted each other, both emotionally and physically. Ayla mentioned she'd been surprised at how fast the bond had formed without her knowing. This must be what she was talking about.

I'm distracted when Malcolm starts climbing the stairs to get to my bedroom. My attention is drawn to his neck. His scent is thick there, so I lean in to drag my tongue from his collarbone to his ear. His hands tighten against my body, and I hear his heart rate pick up. Emboldened, I nibble lightly on his earlobe and gently dig my nails into the back of his neck.

He rewards my efforts with a ragged moan and a low curse.

I'm quickly placed on my feet once we reach the landing, my back pressed to a wall. Dimly, I realize that my purr is still vibrating my chest, but that's not nearly as important as the fact that Malcolm's body is now pressed flush against mine.

"I won't take you for the first time while you're drunk," he rumbles against my ear. "But fuck if I won't taste you before I tuck you into for the night."

My ovaries perk up and scream, "Yes please!" as his head lowers to mine. This kiss isn't soft. This kiss is meant to be a claim, and I liquify against him. Our tongues battle as Malcolm grinds his hips, and a rather large erection, against me. I'm tall enough that I'm able to arch my hips in response and feel him hit just the right spot through my shorts.

I moan into the kiss, tangling my hands in his hair to keep him in place. *Mierda*, I can't get enough of him. He's all I can feel, taste, smell, and see. Our eyes remain open and locked on one another as we battle for dominance with our tongues, but it's not nearly enough. My panther is pacing inside me, wanting to mark her mate to warn off any other females.

I can feel the swirl of his magic flair, and mine leaps joyously to join his. I knew the joining of mates could be intense, but this is another level. I hadn't realized magic could mingle like this, sending pleasant jolts throughout my body.

Malcolm pulls his lips from mine, and I'm mildly embarrassed at the small whimper that escapes me. But I shouldn't have worried. His lips start to trail down my neck as his hand slides down my body, playing with one of my nipples through my thin tank top. My head falls back against the wall as I expose my neck, something shifters only do for mates or alphas. I release his hair to dig my fingers into his shoulders as his hand continues farther south.

Chapter Four

My breathing is ragged as Malcolm snakes his hand into the front of my sleep shorts, and a low moan sounds from both of us as he discovers I'm not wearing anything beneath them.

"Just one fucking taste," he growls against my neck, making me shudder.

"Yes." The thought of his mouth on me...*mierda*. I had no idea just a thought could nearly make me come.

His fingers dance along my clit and my eyes slide closed. I arch my hips to bring his fingers to where I *need* them, but he just continues to lightly circle my clit, torturing me like a bastard. My panther growls threateningly inside me, but when he bites my collarbone, I'm surprised when my panther just melts, once again purring with contentment.

Far too slowly for my liking, Malcolm's finger slides into me. My nails dig deeper into his shoulders as he adds a second digit. He doesn't thrust them into me, instead, he glides the pads of his fingers over my channel...searching.

"Malcolm!" He finds my G-spot at the exact moment his thumb starts to circle my clit. My breath hitches. He gently, slowly, starts to work both spots, almost as though he has all the damn time in the world.

His lips move up to my throat, and his other hand starts to play with my nipple. "You're so hot and wet, Liv." His voice is husky, the timbre causing my pussy to clamp down around his fingers, which only makes him chuckle darkly. "That's right, kitten, squeeze my fingers like you would my cock."

I'm usually not a dirty talk kind of girl, but Malcolm makes it all sound so damn good. The deep, rumbling British accent, combined with the way he's touching me, makes me so damn hot I start panting.

I can feel my orgasm rushing to the surface faster than I would have expected, considering his leisurely pace. I moan loudly, not bothering to hide how good it feels to have him caressing all my good spots at once. Suddenly, he bites down hard on my shoulder. It's not hard enough to break the skin, and certainly not a permanent mate mark, but it's hard enough to have my panther roar inside me as I scream my release.

Still in a daze, I blink my eyes open to find Malcolm's face close to mine, his burning gaze holding me captive. He removes his fingers and slowly brings them to his mouth before licking them clean. A low rumble sounds from him, and his eyes burn brighter as he tastes me. Fuck. Me. That is *hot*.

When he's finished, he leans in to whisper, "The next time you challenge me like that in front of anyone, you had better be ready for me to bend you over and fuck you senseless while they watch."

I'm still dazed from the damn orgasm he managed to get out of me, so it takes a moment for his words to sink in, but once they do, I bristle. I sober right the fuck up too.

"You'd better be ready to make me submit, witch." My

panther adds her own growl to my threat. "Because I will challenge you as much as I want, *pendejo*."

He chuckles darkly as he pulls back to grin at me. "Excellent."

~

THE NEXT MORNING dawns far too soon for my liking. Normally, I'm a morning person—unlike Ayla—but between the witch wine and the super casual hallway orgasm from Malcolm, I just want to stay in bed a bit longer.

His words, his challenge, from last night ring in my mind again, and I bolt upright in bed. That *pendejo* said he would bend me over in front of everyone if I challenged him again. I snort. He can fucking try.

I am sick, *sick*, of all this back and forth with him. I'd bet money he's going to put distance between us this morning, but I'm not going to let him. Between his whole "save the stupid little female" stunt and his comments last night, he's gotten me truly pissed off. If he thinks he can toy with me just because we have a mate bond, he has another thing coming.

Malcolm is about to realize that I am a woman. Ain't no one who does petty like a pissed off woman. An evil grin spreads across my face as the urge to stay in bed vanishes and a new determination flickers to life in my core.

He better bring it.

I get out of bed, choose an outfit to make a grown-ass witch weep, and then get in the shower. I know Malcolm has the room next to mine. I've been practicing with my magic, so I'm curious to see if I can break the sound warding on the rooms. I can't be an evil seductress without throwing out a few surprises, now can I?

I close my eyes to help me concentrate, letting my magic

move slowly away from my body as I try to detect the wards. I fist pump when I feel them. I gradually take down the warding between my room and Malcolm's. While a witch's ability to hear isn't on par with a shifter's senses, their hearing is much better than a human's, so he'll be able to hear me just fine.

I nestle myself against the wall of the shower that is closest to his room and run my hands over my body. I'm not going to fake my reaction by any means, but I may turn up the volume a bit. One of my hands starts to play with my nipples while the other settles with my fingers over my clit. Wanting to ensure Malcolm gets the best auditory show possible, I don't touch my clit just yet. Instead, I focus on tweaking my nipples, letting my moans fill the bathroom as I close my eyes and lose myself in the sensation.

My mind helpfully provides images of Malcolm to aid this little display. I groan as I imagine my nipple in his mouth while his hands run down my body. My fingers start to swirl around my clit, a groan escaping my lips. My movements become faster as I start nearing the edge. I don't need to slip my fingers into myself, I can make myself come just by playing with my nipples and clit with images of Malcolm playing in my mind. My head *thumps* against the shower wall as I noisily moan Malcolm's name while I come.

I instantly slap up the warding again and finish my shower, then I dress quickly and glance in the mirror. With a snap of my fingers, my hair is braided down my back in its typical shieldmaiden-esque style. I adjust the girls a bit to make sure they are attention-getters, and then I turn to look at my ass and legs and smile.

My skinny jeans might as well have been painted on, and they are ultra low-rise, so I made sure to wear a little something lacy underneath, because I plan on flashing my ass at Malcolm every chance I get. The thigh-high, black leather boots give my ass a little extra oomph, thanks to the heel. I'm wearing a long-sleeved shirt with a neckline that plunges down to my navel, showing off parts of my bra. It's one of those bras that has all those sinfully sexy straps in the front. I paint on some eyeliner and mascara and head out the door.

A grin spreads across my face when I hear Malcolm's door open right as I begin to descend the stairs. His footsteps falter when he catches sight of me watching him over my shoulder. His eyes smolder, and there's a very clear bulge in his pants. I wink at him and head downstairs.

Malcolm catches up to me halfway down and grabs my arm. I glance down at it and then up into his eyes, arching my eyebrow at him.

"Don't think I'm going to let your little show this morning slide—or this outfit, for that matter." His gaze rakes over me, and I shiver. There's a predatory gleam in his eyes that has my panther panting. "I don't know what the hell you're playing at, Liv, but make no mistake—"

"Don't try to threaten me with a good time, Malcolm," I purr. "You need to make up your mind. Do you want me and this bond or not? The whole 'saving me from myself' bullshit is just that, bullshit. You either want me or you don't." I pull my arm away and keep walking down the stairs. "Now, we both have somewhere to be."

As I enter the dining room, I notice that Ayla and Caleb are already there, along with a few of the other Council lackeys we brought with us. Everyone is deep in conversation, but it's nothing serious by the sounds of it, so I take my time getting myself some breakfast and coffee. Malcolm stalks into the room, shooting a glare at me as he roughly takes a seat with his arms crossed.

"Well, okay, big guy," Ayla starts. "What the hell has your panties in a knot?" Her gaze flicks between Malcolm and me, as though she's trying to solve the world's most difficult puzzle.

"I don't think you need to be delving into their personal affairs, Ayla." Ayla turns to level a glare at Caleb, as though the mere thought of not being involved in my personal affairs is offensive to her.

I choke down a laugh.

I decide to change the subject. "What were you guys talking about when I walked in?" Ayla is going to corner me when we're alone anyway, no need to discuss this in front of everyone.

Ayla casts me a narrow-eyed look before answering, "We were talking about visiting the Council's library to see if there's any information about the prophecy itself. But first, we wanted to search my parents' cottage. It's something I feel should not be done with a bunch of random people around." She throws that last part at Caleb.

"Why don't you and I tackle the cottage? We can take a small group with us, and they can stay outside like the good guards they are. Malcolm and Caleb can head to the library." I don't miss the glare either male aims in my direction, but given Ayla's huge grin, I know we'll get our way.

"You need to keep the bond open at all times," Caleb growls. Ayla nods her agreement and starts to guzzle another cup of coffee.

"Olivia," Malcolm growls in a low warning, "let's talk alone for a minute."

"Let's not." I shoot a tight-lipped smile his way as I start in on my coffee.

"That wasn't a request."

"I'm a queen, Malcolm. I don't take orders from you." My panther growls her agreement with me, and I allow my eyes to flash over the rim of my coffee cup when I look at him again.

Fine. We'll talk like this. Malcolm sounds annoyed, and I can't stop myself from rolling my eyes. Poor, sweet, fragile man. *You shouldn't be going anywhere near that cottage. Not after what happened yesterday.*

Look, I told you earlier, you need to figure your shit out. Stop acting hot one minute and cold the next. Once you determine what the hell you want to do, we can talk about things like partners. Until then, keep your damn opinions to yourself. I slam the bond shut.

~

LATER THAT DAY, Ayla and I are sitting at the table in her parents' cottage, trying to decide where to start. While the cottage is small, it's clear there's magic everywhere, and we aren't sure if that magic is hiding something or simply part of the history of this place. It's going to take us a while to unravel everything.

"So," Ayla starts, "what's going on with you and Malcolm?"

"He's all over me one second, and the next, he's telling me he's staying away from me for my own good." I huff and cross my arms over my chest. "You don't make a woman come all over your fingers in the hallway of some random castle and then act like nothing happened."

"Oh?" She grins over at me. "I was unaware of the finger banging in the hallway."

"Last night. And because he seems to think I'm just going to roll over and show my belly, I took the sound ward off the wall between our rooms and flicked the ole bean in the shower this morning." I grin back at her. "Loudly."

Ayla throws her head back and laughs, which causes me to start laughing too.

"I love that you're such a petty bitch. This is why we're friends." She sighs before giving me a stern look. "Don't make the same mistake I did. Don't push him away."

"I'm not planning on it, but he needs to figure his shit out. I refuse to be a damn yo-yo." I begin tugging on the end of my braid. "But I sure as shit don't plan on making this easy for him either."

"That's my girl."

"We should probably start trying to unravel all the magic in here, huh?" I gesture to the room around us.

"Why do you have to bring rational thought and responsibility into this conversation? I'm trying to avoid thinking about how difficult this is going to be." She shoots a glare at me. "But you're right. We need to think of a way to get through all of this."

Almost of their own volition, our eyes drift back to the symbol on the mantel. It showed us pieces of the puzzle yesterday, so perhaps there are more symbols carved around the house.

"It's a place to start anyway." I'm not even mad that she read my thoughts through our pack bond. "I'll take my parents' room if you'll start out here?"

"Sure. I know you didn't get a chance to go in there yesterday. Do you want me to step out and just give you a minute?"

"No. I'd rather have you close. This is going to be an emotionally draining day." Ayla stood and walked into her parents' room, not bothering to close the door.

I start running my hands over the table, trying to feel for any carvings in the wood. Even if there are other symbols like the one on the mantel, they may not be as easily visible. My mind starts to wander as I continue my search, reflecting on what we witnessed yesterday.

Lucifer went to anchor the prison for the Härja. If recent lore is to be believed, Lucifer is the ruler of Hell. So those seven dark creatures are imprisoned in Hell with Lucifer. Who voluntarily left. Didn't Darcy say she was changed by

Lucifer?

There are so many missing pieces to this puzzle that it's hard to even get a vague understanding of the completed picture. A timeline would be good. I send the mental note to Kelly since she's also eyeballs deep in research and would probably do a better job of the task anyway.

Getting up from the table, I make my way over to the beds tucked in the corner. I poke my head underneath and notice a small wooden box. My hands start to close around the box when I feel the call of magic surge through my veins.

Chapter Five

The magic washes over me, and it feels the same as the energy that surrounded the design on the mantel. My fingers tingle as I pull the box out from under the bed.

The design is engraved here too.

"Ayla!" I don't want to release the box, even after I've placed it reverently on the bed. Ayla's footsteps seem to echo around me as the magic comes to a crescendo.

But before anything else happens, the world goes dark again. An alarm starts shrieking around us, and I feel the magic pull away from me.

I'm on my feet as quickly as possible. Ayla stubs her toe next to me, but I can't see her.

"Something's going on," Ayla yells over the blaring alarm. The noise has my ears ringing and my head spinning. "We need to get to the door."

I feel for her hand, grasping it tightly once we finally make contact. Thankfully, Ayla seems to be moving in the direction of the door. Once we reach it, we pause to take deep breaths.

"I'm not sure what we're going to see once we walk out this door. Are you ready?" Ayla's voice is quiet but laced with steel.

"Girl, I was born ready."

Ayla jerks the door open, and we step out into the clearing around the cottage. Light floods our senses, blinding us for a brief moment. When my eyes adjust, the scene before me takes a moment to sink in. The supernaturals we brought with us are all dead, and roughly two hundred demons have formed a semicircle around the front of the cottage.

So going dark and screaming at us is the cottage's way of telling us to stay inside. Good to know.

I glance over at Ayla, and our gazes lock. She nods. She already told Caleb what's going on, but we're going to need to fight until they can get here. We shift at the same time.

My panther, the bloodthirsty kitty she is, is ready to rip them limb from limb. Our wings, still untested, stretch before tucking in tightly against our back.

I don't sense an archdemon, do you? I'm new at the whole queen thing, so I want to make sure I'm not overlooking anything.

No. Oddly enough, I don't sense one either. Well, okay then. This isn't sketchy as all hell or anything.

My claws dig into the ground as a low growl rumbles through my chest. I'm eyeing the demons in front of us when Ayla bursts into the sky. The sudden movement seems to take the demons by surprise, which is all the opening I need as I launch myself at them.

As I rip into the demons around me, it dawns on me that Malcolm and Caleb aren't here yet. They should have been able to portal here by now.

What's taking Caleb and Malcolm so long?

Something is preventing them from opening a portal. They're going to try a bit farther out and then fly here.

Shit.

I have no idea how long that will take them, but it'll be too long. Despite Ayla wielding the elements against the demons, and my panther ripping every single one of them to shreds, we're not making a dent in the horde. A sharp pain pierces my side, making me falter as my panther growls and we take in the threat around us.

I can't get a good enough look at my side to determine the extent of the damage, but I can feel blood matting my fur. The wound feels deep, and I know I'm running out of time—soon I'll be of no use in this fight.

The earth rumbles beneath my feet as Ayla attempts to bury as many demons as she can. I shake my head, digging my claws into the dirt to ground me. I allow my magic to swell within me. Maybe I can turn a few inside out.

Just as I'm about to unleash my magic, Ayla's stunned voice carries through our pack bond. *Oh fuck me sideways. Liv...Look up.*

My instincts scream at me as I rip my gaze from the threat in front of me, only to be confronted with a new aerial threat.

I thought only archdemons could fly. What the hell am I seeing?

They certainly aren't archdemons. Ayla's dragon swoops over me before soaring toward whatever it is that's coming at us from the sky. *I won't get too close, but I need to figure out what we're dealing with.*

Just keep the bond open. I don't waste any more time worrying about what's heading toward us, turning my focus back to the demons in front of me.

It's times like these when I really wish I learned to fly before now. Fucking up a large group of the demons would be much easier. Originally, there appeared to be roughly two hundred or so, but more keep coming, and it doesn't feel like we've even made a dent in their numbers.

I release my hold on my magic, and a group of demons in front of me explode, splattering me with guts and gore. Ick. My blood is still seeping from my side, making the ground beneath my paws slick. I feel a sense of lethargy that only accompanies blood loss starting to weave its way through my consciousness. *Mierda.*

Liv, I don't think Katia was just experimenting with shifter females. Ayla's tone is filled with dread. *They've given lower-level demons wings.*

You have got to be kidding me! Seriously? Is it too much to ask for an even playing field? Another blow makes it past my defenses and cuts into my chest. Apparently, it is too much to ask for.

Ayla lands next to me, still in her dragon form. *They're clumsy and it'll take a while for them to get here, but I doubt we'll be finished with these guys before they arrive.* She inhales. *Shit, Liv, you're injured. Are you okay?*

I have to be, don't I? My response is a little testier than I would like, but pain is radiating throughout my body, and the additional blood loss is messing with my head. *Where the hell are the others?*

They're coming. Malcolm is riding on Caleb. They portaled as close as they could. They should be here soon. I'm not leaving your side, lady. She lashes out at any demon who dares to get too close.

I can feel my hold on my shift slipping, and the urge to change into my human form is exceedingly strong. Although I've been training to use my magic for a while now, I don't feel nearly as comfortable relying on it as I do with my shifter abilities. I'm faster and more powerful in my panther form, but it looks like I'm not going to have much of a choice.

Moments later, the shift is forced on me, and I painfully transform back into my human body.

"I can't remember the last time the shift hurt that much." The wound on my side is worse in my human form. I curse demon wounds and their interference with our usual fast healing. The slice on my chest is also worse than it appeared, deeper and more jagged.

Stay alert. Ayla's sharp response echoes in my head. *I'm going to keep as much of them off you as I can. They just keep coming. You need to use your magic.*

Taking a deep breath to center myself, I allow my magic to swell within me again. She's right. I'm going to need to fight for as long as possible. Twin balls of flame appear above my hands. I like to think it's due to my spicy Latina personality, because fire was the first and easiest element for me to master.

AYLA AND I have been fighting to keep the demons off us for what feels like hours. My flames are starting to flicker out, and the lethargy I was feeling earlier is threatening to consume me entirely, but the aerial legion is almost upon us.

I'm going to need to tell Ayla to leave me here.

Like fucking hell. My mental walls must be down if she heard me. I glance over at her.

She's also covered in blood. Most of it belongs to the demons, but some of it's her own. My legs give way, and I slam onto my knees, the impact jarring me enough that my flames sputter out completely.

"I'd really prefer we didn't both die here." I try to keep my tone light, but the glare she cuts me, even as a dragon, is enough to send ice down my spine.

Ayla shifts back into her human form, slamming her foot

on the ground to erect a large wall of earth between us and the demons. Why the hell didn't we do that earlier?

"It's not going to hold for long," Ayla warns as if reading my mind again. "I'm worried if we go back into the cottage for protection, they'll be able to breach the wards. They know too much about this place."

I agree. The fact that they could even track us here is alarming, but I can't seem to find the energy to form the words, so I let my thoughts drift through the bond.

Ayla kneels beside me, slinging my arm around her shoulders. "Caleb and Malcolm are just cresting the hill. They are taking on the aerial demons to get to us. The others are right behind them. Hang on, Liv."

I try. Man, do I try. But my world goes dark moments later.

～

"MAMA! MAMA!" My little legs pump to get me into the house as fast as possible. "There is a woman here to see you, Mama!"

I skid to a halt in our kitchen, my mother humming happily as she sits at the table, kneading dough. I take a moment just to look at her and bask in her glow. There's always been something about my mama that just seems to shimmer and shine. She's one of the most beautiful women I've ever seen. I'm only eight, but I know there is something different about Mama, something not all other shifters have.

"Who is it, mija?" My mother continues to knead the bread dough, glancing up at me as her hands press and squeeze.

"She says she needs your help." I scramble up onto the wooden chair beside her.

Her hands pause, and her face tightens. My spine tingles. Mama is not happy this woman is here.

She stands, wiping her hands on a cloth at her waist. "Stay here, mija. Do not come outside."

Of course I cannot help but quietly follow behind her. I want to know who this woman is who makes Mama this unhappy.

"I told you not to come here."

"I know." The woman's accent is funny. "But I'm running out of time. My girls need to go into hiding. Now. I need to know if you've seen anything about the locations I've given you."

"You are surrounded by darkness and death. I do not want that near my daughter." Mama's voice is laced with power and rage. "I told you that I would meet you in the village tomorrow."

"There isn't time. I swear." The woman sounds frantic. "Please, I need to know."

Mama huffs out a breath, still angry. "Sit down." There's the sound of shuffling feet before Mama continues, "One of your daughters, the youngest, won't make it into hiding. If you don't tamper with her memory, lock away parts of what she is. They will find her shortly after they take you, and they will take you. Only you."

The scent of tears wafts through the air, salty and strong.

"If you do as I say, they will all live."

~

THE MEMORY STARTS to fade as my eyes flutter open. The implication of what I just saw leaves me shaken, and I hardly notice the throb in my side or my chest. My mother was a seer. Mama was a seer and she helped Aine. I needed to tell Ayla as soon as possible.

"Thank fuck." Malcolm's deep timbre reaches me as I blink a few times to clear the fog from my mind. "Thank *fuck*."

His hand envelops mine as my gaze slides to his face. He's pale, and he has dark circles around his eyes. His hair is a disaster, and I'm pretty sure his shirt isn't buttoned right. What the hell happened to him?

It takes me a moment to remember what happened, and

as soon as I do, the throbbing in my chest and side come blazing back to the forefront of my mind.

"Was that even Spanish?" Malcolm's lips twitch after I've finished cursing. "It was so fast and furious, I'm not sure what language any of that was in."

"Spanglish, *pendejo.*" He chuckles softly at my response. "What happened?"

"Well," he starts, "after you passed out, Ayla was able to hold that earth wall just long enough for Caleb and me to make it to the edge of that demon swarm. They left pretty quickly after we arrived though. We're betting this was just a test of our resources."

Wait a minute. "Are you telling me I was taken out by a *scouting* party?" I realize the rage I feel is probably a tad irrational, but...a scouting party? Have I lost my groove? Maybe I should just hand myself over to Malick.

"I wouldn't call them a scouting party. They certainly knew some of the core group is here, but they weren't sure what that meant until today." The laughter is gone from his face, and he's looking me over a bit more closely now. "How are you feeling? The wounds were deep. Frankly, I'm surprised you're awake. I've only done two healing sessions on you."

"Today? I haven't been out longer?" My brain is a bit slow on the uptake right now. "That doesn't make any sense."

Malcolm doesn't suppress his chuckle this time. "It's been about three hours." I must look exceptionally confused, because he continues, "You're not well enough to get up and move around. I'm just bloody happy you're awake at all. I assumed you'd be out for at least another day or so."

I go to shift, but the pain lancing through my core stops me, and I suck in a breath. "Well, I'm certainly still in pain." I glance down at my torso, but I can't see anything except some white bandages above the hem of my tank top. I'm covered in a light blanket and shorts too.

"I'll go get you something for the pain and let the others know you're awake. Ayla may just sucker punch Caleb if he doesn't let her in here, so I'll give you two a minute." He stands, his eyes darkening. "I'm not letting you out of my sight."

I roll my eyes. Men. "Okay, *pendejo*. Just get me something for the pain so I can rest again."

He winks at me before leaving the room.

Chapter Six

I groan loudly when the sun's rays stab into my closed eyes the next morning. The pain isn't as bad as it was yesterday, more a dull throbbing than the searing heat I had to deal with before. I groan as my eyes flutter open. I'd much rather drag the covers over my head and rest for an eternity than get out of bed, but I know that isn't an option right now. I need to talk to the others about what happened and what the plan is.

A dip in the mattress has my head turning as my eyes attempt to focus. Ayla is sitting on the side of the bed. She's in yoga pants and a tank top, so she probably just woke up herself—if she slept at all. I know her too well to assume that she got the rest she needed while I was out of commission, even though we talked yesterday and I assured her I was going to be just fine.

"I'm sorry I left you to fend for yourself out there. I shouldn't have stayed in the air so long," she murmurs, shame lacing her tone.

"Hey," I retort sharply, "don't do that to yourself. You were able to take out more demons from above. It's not your fault I haven't learned how to fly yet."

Ayla's eyes are tortured as they bore into mine. "That's not a good enough excuse, Olivia, and you know it." She pinches the bridge of her nose before continuing, "I should have had your back."

"You *did* have my back, woman. That's what I'm trying to say." Annoyance has me sitting up and grabbing her hand. "We had no idea when the others were going to get to us. Destroying as many of them as possible was the right call."

She shakes her head, her eyes hard as they take me in. "No. The right call would have been to have us go back into the cottage."

"And get roasted alive?" I scoff. "Right. We had no idea if they would be able to get in or if they would just set fire to the whole damn thing with us inside. I'd rather go out fighting than trapped in a burning building, and so would you."

I understand her worry. I do. But to have all this guilt is ridiculous, and if she was able to think clearly, she would know that. We knew Malick would find another mage, and we should have assumed he already had one on reserve. There would always be someone willing to do unspeakable things for power. We should have taken extra precautions. We'd been lulled into a false sense of security these past few weeks. It was just as much my fault as anyone else's.

As Ayla's beta, it was my duty to take care of security, so technically, I'm the one who failed her. I didn't consider all the possibilities. I was too caught up in the changes I've been going through to stop and think more critically about our safety.

Sure, we have the Council with us, but that doesn't give me permission to slack off on my duties to Ayla and the community.

I rub a hand down my face, sighing loudly. "Look. I should have anticipated an attack and planned accordingly. I didn't. I'm the one who got people killed, Ayla. It's my job to take care of these things, so cut the crap." My rebuke is harsh, and she blinks in surprise at my tone.

"Liv—"

"No," I cut her off. "You know I'm right. You think you need to be in charge of everything, but we both know that's not true. I'm your beta, security is part of my job. We got caught with our damn pants around our ankles. But it's *not* your fault I was injured."

She huffs out a breath. "You're a pain in the ass, you know that?"

"Yes," I state proudly. "I do."

With a laugh, Ayla throws her arms around my shoulders and hugs me tightly. I bask in the comfort her hug provides, sliding my arms around her just as snugly.

"Did they attack at home too?" I didn't feel anything through the pack bond to suggest any of the shifters at home were fighting or injured, but I still need to be sure.

"No, thank the goddess," she replies with relief. Thank the goddess indeed.

Caleb's amused tone floats to us from the door. "I hate to break up the love fest, but Malcolm needs to look over Olivia to make sure everything is healing as it should."

He saunters into the room, Malcolm slinking in behind him. We pull apart, my gaze narrowing on Malcolm. He's got his hands in his pockets, and he's watching me in a manner that unnerves the crap out of me. Ayla takes my hand as she turns toward them, and that touch keeps me grounded.

"I'm fine. I swear." I look at them pointedly. "You're all overbearing mother hens."

"We care about you." Ayla gives me a sharp look in return

before raising a brow in Malcolm's direction. I fight not to roll my eyes in response.

"Come on, love." Caleb takes Ayla's hand, giving me a quick once over himself to make sure I really am okay. "You scared us, Liv."

"Sorry about that." I tuck my hair behind my ear, feeling awkward at Caleb's show of emotion. "I'm assuming once I get a clean bill of health, we'll meet to go over what happened...with food?" I send them my best puppy dog eyes.

Caleb chuckles before responding, "Yes. We'll meet in the war room and go over everything. I'll make sure there is plenty of food. I know how much a healing shifter eats."

"Bless you."

He chuckles again before dragging Ayla out of the room.

My gaze goes back to Malcolm, who's standing a few feet from my bed, his hands still in his pockets. I slide off the mattress, and his eyes track every move I make.

"I feel a lot better than I did yesterday." I hold my arms out at my sides and spin slowly. I'm in a pair of shorts, and my chest is covered by the bandage that's over my wound. "I haven't even bled through my bandages."

"I can see that." His eyes are heated when my gaze meets his again. He steps up to me, closer than he needs to for an inspection of my injuries. His hands, glowing softly with his magic, roam over my body, not quite touching, but I'm hyper-aware of them nonetheless.

"Malcolm." My voice is breathy. I'm not even sure what I want to say.

He steps into me, resting his hands on my hips. He mumbles something I can't quite make out before resting his forehead against mine. We stay like that for a heartbeat, two, three. Something shifts between us, solidifies.

"You're almost fully healed, which is a small miracle." His eyes close and he swallows. "Liv..." His voice is hoarse. "When we got to you—Christ. You shouldn't have survived the blood loss alone."

His words sink into me and ice rushes through my veins. I'd known I was losing a lot of blood, but I hadn't realized just how much. Goddess. I search his face. His eyes are still closed, as though the thought of me bleeding out is just too much to face right now, and that's when I realize what's changed between us. We may continue to dance around each other, but he almost lost me. He doesn't want to lose me.

I cradle his cheeks in my hands, and his eyes snap open. "Malcolm, I wasn't about to give up out there. We've got too much between us right now for me to just casually die."

Malcolm's rough laugh, startled out of him, brings a smile to my face. "Casually die, she says." He shakes his head in exasperation, gently enough that my hands don't leave his cheeks. "There was nothing casual about yesterday."

He takes one of my hands and presses a kiss to my palm. I feel that kiss all the way to my toes.

"You can take the bandages off your chest and side. You're healed enough, so you don't need them. Get dressed. I'll meet you in the war room."

Now it's my turn to laugh. I'd forgotten Caleb had mentioned a war room. "You guys really have a war room? I thought he was kidding."

"It's legit, kitten." My panther bristles at the endearment. "It's the first door on the right after the kitchen." With that, he leaves me to get ready.

I take a moment to just breathe. Drunken karaoke with Ayla feels like years ago, not two nights prior. How did Ayla handle all of this? It's overwhelming. I know I'm not alone, but that isn't exactly the point. Having a support system to help is so important, and it's what's gotten me through up until now, but they aren't able to process or deal with everything for me. They can provide love and encouragement, but I'm ultimately the one who has to do the heavy lifting.

No one can make me feel anything. They are my emotions. I need to own them, which I'm usually pretty good at. The problem right now is that I don't even know what I'm feeling. Too much, I'm feeling too much.

I now understand why Malcolm wanted to give us time, my panther rumbles. A part of me wants to bitch slap her, but she's right. I had a good handle on things until we hauled ass here to Ireland.

But he shouldn't be part of the problem. He should be part of the solution, I reply, and she doesn't argue. As our mate, Malcolm should be here to help with things like this. Not with owning my emotions, but with sorting out how I feel, just as I should be there for him.

Admittedly, him holding back from the bond, from me, is causing more harm than good. I'm just not sure how to explain that to him in a way that will make him get his head out of his ass.

MAKING my way to the war room is easy, just as Malcolm said it would be. Getting into the room, however, is a different beast. I can feel the magic radiating off the door before I'm even in front of it. This room is warded to high heaven.

Taking the opportunity to test out my new magic detection abilities, I pause in the hallway, letting my magic free. It reaches across the space and caresses the wards around the door. I'm not entirely sure how my magic tells me, but it communicates that the energy won't hurt me since it's been keyed to me, but if it wasn't, it would burn me to a crisp. Good to know.

The magic warding the door eases, allowing me to pass,

and my magic curls back inside me. The door opens smoothly, and the room before me has my jaw dropping.

The size of a ballroom with vaulted ceilings, the war room has one wall that's floor to ceiling windows with French doors that lead out to a stunningly beautiful garden. The wall opposite the windows has a world map that's been enchanted, and there are tiny glowing dots all over it. I'm not sure if it shows all known supernaturals or Council bases. The wall farthest the door has a floor to ceiling bookshelf and is completely filled with tomes. The vaulted ceiling boasts two glittering chandeliers, and the floors are a white marble with black and gold veins running randomly throughout. The most impressive item in the room, however, is the table that commands most of the floor. It's a shimmering black onyx with plush, high-backed chairs evenly spaced around its circumference. The table itself, while beautiful, holds the most intricate piece of magic I've ever seen.

It's a three-dimensional casting of the area around the cottage. I assume it can show similar images of everyplace on the planet. It feels as though I've stepped into a futuristic, science fiction, galaxy traveling novel. It's not a hologram, it's solid, and it appears to be playing Ayla's memories of the battle we fought yesterday.

I want one.

"I'll let you play with it if you promise not to drool all over it." A tinkling laugh reaches me and shakes me out of my stupor. "It's not that hard to master."

The witch before me is tiny, about the same height as Ayla, and she's slender, almost elven in appearance. She's got a cute pixie cut that's dyed a shocking hot pink. Her eyes are a unique shade of violet, and she's got a wide grin on her face.

"I'm Fayden!" She holds out her hand, and I shake it. "I'm the head of tech for the Council."

"I feel like 'head of tech' is extremely misleading, Fay."

Malcolm comes over to stand next to her. "She's got an insane ability to combine magic and technology." He shakes his head. "She's also my sister and she's only fifteen."

Fayden sticks her tongue out at Malcolm, crossing her arms as she mockingly glares at him. "I like head of tech. It sounds mature." Malcolm chuckles.

"I'm Olivia." I smile at Fayden, purposely ignoring Malcolm. "I'll refer to you by whatever you want if you get me one of those at home." She grins. "Especially if it'll annoy your brother."

"Deal." She looks at Malcolm, triumph glittering in her eyes. "Finally, I don't need to get your approval to go somewhere."

Malcolm just shakes his head and musses her hair before winking at me and turning back to the table. Fayden looks mildly annoyed and completely exasperated.

"It's also able to show different future scenarios as needed. There's also a magical A.I. component that tries to calculate future events. The more information we put in it, the better it's able to make predictions."

If I didn't need one before, I absolutely need one now. "Did I mention that I need it?" We laugh. "I'm seriously impressed, Fayden. If you ever want to ditch your embarrassing brother, you can totally come work for me."

Her eyes go comically wide. She stares at me the way I'm gazing at the display over the table. I meant every word. I'm more than happy to have her join the community. We seem to be continuing the trend of having women in positions of power, and I see no need to stop.

"I heard that!" Malcolm calls. "Careful what you wish for, Liv. She's a menace."

I roll my eyes and loop my arm through Fayden's. "He says the same thing about me."

Chapter Seven

We're all settled around the onyx table when Fayden asks me to place my hand on a circular crystal that appears in front of me. "It'll take your memories of the events leading up to and during the battle, which will help the A.I. extrapolate potential futures."

Ayla looks at Fayden like she's some sort of unicorn. "And you're only fifteen?" When Fayden grins, Ayla groans softly. "I've been alive for almost five hundred years, but you've done so much more with your life than I have. I'm mildly jealous."

"Don't be," I chirp. "Her brother is Malcolm. I wouldn't wish that on anyone."

Ayla giggles, and Malcolm glowers at me.

"I'll have you know I am an *excellent* older brother," Malcolm scoffs.

Fayden snorts and covers her mouth behind her hand.

"I am!"

"It's going to take a while before we'll get anything from the system," Fayden informs us with a small smile. "I can let you all know when it's ready."

Malcolm pops out of his seat surprisingly quickly. "Great."

He grabs hold of my hand, dragging me out of my chair. "I have something I need to talk to Olivia about."

I quirk my eyebrow at him but allow myself to be led away. I hear Ayla chuckling behind us. I don't bother to say anything until we're standing in front of the door to my room.

"What is going on?"

"We have unfinished business," is all he says as he opens the door, ushers me inside, and then closes it, warding it with a wave of his hand.

"Do we now?" I can't contain my smirk. "What business is that?"

He doesn't answer, just backs me into the wall near the door. His eyes darken as he places his hands on either side of my head, effectively boxing me in. I lift a brow at him, waiting to see what he does instead of taking the lead myself.

"You said you didn't need time when it came to the bond," he growls as he lowers his head to nip my neck, causing me to shiver.

"I did," I confirm in a breathy voice, which is mildly embarrassing. My panther stills inside me, and I can feel my eyes shift into cat eyes.

His mouth descends on mine, fierce, hot, and so full of passion that it steals my breath. I arch into him, threading my fingers in his hair. He groans when my tongue touches his. His hands move from the wall, one fisting in my hair to move my head into a better angle, the other sliding down my body to grasp my ass. Malcolm kneads the flesh in an almost desperate manner, then nips my lip before licking away the sting.

He pulls me firmly against his body, and I feel the evidence of his arousal pressed against my lower stomach. The hand that was tangled in my hair vanishes for a moment, then the sharp snap of his fingers jolts me out of my lust fueled haze. I start to move my head back, but Malcolm's hand tangles in my hair again, keeping our lips fused.

We're both naked.

The thought registers a moment before Malcolm's hand squeezes my ass again. Not needing any further encouragement, I hop up, wrap my legs around him, and tighten my arms around his shoulders at the same time, my hands still buried in his hair.

I'm going to mark you, kitten. I'll be balls deep inside you, and you'll be screaming my name when I do it.

I moan into his mouth. I'm so ready.

Malcolm keeps me pressed against the wall, our bodies practically fused together, and shifts his hand from my ass to my thigh. We're too close for his hand to slide the precious few inches to my clit. Which, while mildly disappointing, isn't necessary. I'm already wet enough to drown a damn mermaid.

Play later. Get that dick in me. Now.

A soft chuckle is his response. He lifts his head slightly, and I open my eyes, both of us panting for breath. "I want to see your face when I fill your sweet pussy."

Mierda, this man is a dirty talker, and I am here for it.

My lips part on a groan as his cock bumps my clit before easing into me. The man has girth. It stings a bit as he thrusts home, burying himself to the hilt, but damn if that sting doesn't feel amazing.

Malcolm's head falls to my shoulder as he remains still inside me. How sweet, he's giving me time to adjust—time I don't need nor want. I start rolling my hips, angling to take him deeper. A soft grunt meets my ear before he withdraws, pausing for a moment before slamming home again.

Yes. This. I don't want soft and sweet for our first time. I've been craving him for far too long. I need it fast and hard.

I try to tell him that through our bond, but all I manage is a moan as he continues his assault.

He moves slightly, allowing his fingers to access my clit, and my head thumps back against the wall, my breath hitching as he starts caressing it. I can feel my orgasm barreling toward me, my pussy clenching tightly around Malcolm's cock.

"That's right, kitten," Malcolm growls into my neck. "Milk my cock."

My panther roars to the forefront of my mind, and I feel my teeth shift in anticipation of marking him as our mate. Malcolm starts to nibble my neck, his own orgasm rapidly approaching as well. The feeling of his teeth against my flesh is all I need to detonate like a nuclear bomb.

I scream out my release as my teeth sink into the junction of Malcolm's neck and shoulder. His teeth pierce my neck a moment later, a low groan rumbling in his throat from his own release. The mate bond that had been so thin snaps into place, allowing our emotions to flood into each other.

Malcolm is damn pleased to finally make this official. While witches don't bite their mates like shifters normally do, he did it purely on instinct. Witches typically exchange their magic with their mate, though the exact details are unknown to me. When he bit me, Malcolm made sure some of his magic flooded into me through the wound, sealing us together not just in the traditional shifter way, but in the witch way as well.

The thought made my heart melt. He wanted us bound in every way possible.

Settling both his hands on my ass, Malcolm moved me over to my bed, putting me down carefully before going into the bathroom.

I hear the water in the tub running when Malcolm comes back out. He grins at me before scooping me up off the bed and carrying me into the bathroom where I see a bubble bath has been started.

"Is that for me?" I blink up at him happily.

"It's for us." He leans down to peck my lips before sliding us both into the tub. It's not completely full, so the water is still running, but it feels amazing anyway.

We sit in silence until the tub fills and Malcolm stops the water with a flick of his wrist. I slide against him, feeling him harden as I do. He leans down to nibble on my ear, but he doesn't make a move to do more while we soak.

"Not that I'm complaining," I start, "but why now?"

"You almost died." Malcolm's voice is quiet. He leans his head back against the edge of the tub and closes his eyes, as if reliving the moment he and Caleb arrived at the battle. "There was so much blood. I wasn't sure we'd gotten to you in time. The bond was so damn quiet."

I can feel his anguish through the bond, so I cuddle closer to him, sliding my arms around him to hold him close. I know if I found him in a similar position I'd be devastated. Hell, I can't even think about him like that without feeling my heart rate pick up.

"I didn't want to regret not bonding with you, so I promised myself that if you made it out alright, I would complete the mate bond." His eyes open and he presses a soft kiss to my temple.

"Well, now you're stuck with me." My attempt at lightening the mood is forced, but thankfully, Malcolm smiles.

"I hope you're rested, kitten," he says huskily.

"Oh?" My heart skips a beat as I look into his eyes, which have darkened with desire.

"You're not going to get much rest for the remainder of the day, Liv." He grins. "In fact, you're going to need to rest up tomorrow if I have any say."

"Oh, you adorable witch." I grin. "You're the one who is going to need rest tomorrow."

It's the middle of the night when something jars me awake. A dream? A memory? I rub my temples as I try to concentrate. Malcolm is dead to the world, curled up behind me with one arm wrapped tightly around my middle and one leg over both of mine. His warmth lulls me back into a relaxed sleepy state, but the nagging that something's not quite right doesn't go away, and I can't seem to close my eyes for long.

It feels as though I've forgotten something. But what?

My eyelids are heavy and I'm trying to drift back off to sleep, but my heart starts racing again and I can't seem to slow it down.

"Liv?" Malcolm's sleep roughened voice sends shivers down my spine. "What's wrong? I can feel your anxiety through the bond." He hugs me closer.

"I'm...not sure," I murmur. "Something woke me up, and now I feel like I've forgotten something. Something important."

Malcolm shifts so he's leaning over me, scanning my face. "Were you dreaming?"

"I don't think so." His brows draw down in confusion. "It's just such a weird feeling. It won't go away."

He leans down to press a kiss to my throat and my eyes slide shut. I can feel him searching the bond to see if he can uncover whatever is just out of my reach. One of his hands starts to draw little circles on my chest, stirring my hunger for him and shoving whatever discontent I was feeling to the side.

"Malcolm." My tone is husky with desire.

"Hmm?" His eyes are hooded, and his fingers start to

wander toward my nipple. "I can't tell what's wrong, so I figured I'd try to take your mind off it to help you get to sleep."

I bite my lip, both to prevent myself from smiling and to keep myself from groaning. My body shifts of its own accord, leaning into his chest. Malcolm's finger circles my nipple, not ready to give me what I want.

"We can think about what could be bothering you in the morning. Caleb told me the system is ready to show us some of the outcomes it was able to predict, so maybe that will help jog your memory." His finger just brushes my nipple and my breath whooshes out of me.

"That will work," I murmur breathlessly, and my back arches in an attempt to get him to actually touch me.

He pulls back, his eyes dark with desire. "How many orgasms do you think you'll need before you can relax?" A smirk spreads across his face.

"Good question." I tap my chin in thought. "At least three, possibly more."

"Your wish is my command." His whispered words cause me to shiver with anticipation.

Malcolm gently nibbles on my ear before starting his journey south, worshipping my body as he goes. He bites down gently on my collarbone, which incites my panther to release a rumbling purr. Chuckling softly, he finally makes it to my breasts.

My breath hitches when he blows softly on my nipples, and I bite down on my lip to prevent me from whimpering in need. He's not touching me anywhere else, and it's driving me insane. I begin to tug his mouth to me, but his magic flares and my hands slam onto the bed.

"I'm sorry, kitten" —Malcolm's eyes flick up to mine— "but I'm in charge here."

Miedra.

"Now let me get back to work."

"Sir, yes, sir!"

His eyes narrow before he once again focuses on my chest. I may be in trouble. Malcolm kisses between my breasts, running his nose along the tender flesh there. He's going to tease me. Rude. His lips brush just beyond my nipple, causing me to groan. I feel the smirk he's wearing, and I want to smack it off him.

A gentle caress works its way from my sides to my thighs, and my legs part as if they have a mind of their own. He's touching me, but it's so light that it only serves to frustrate me instead of sate me.

"Malcolm," I snarl. He only chuckles in response.

Karma is a bitch, *pendejo*.

Malcolm's tongue flicks out against my nipple, too fast to really count for anything. They are hard and aching, and I just need some form of pressure there to relieve the ache. He leans over to the other hardened tip, flicking it a few times with just the tip of his tongue. My back arches in an attempt to get closer to his mouth.

Just as I'm trying to figure out how to break the magic holding my hands to the bed so I can smother the insufferable witch on top of me, he finally, *finally*, takes me into his mouth. His fingers slip down to circle my clit at the exact same moment.

"It's about damn time!" He pauses. "If you want to live to see tomorrow, you won't stop."

His body shakes as he laughs, but instead of stopping, he continues with gusto and I'm soon panting his name. Malcolm's fingers curl gently, rubbing against my G-spot. My back bows off the mattress, and my eyes slide closed as waves of pleasure rack my body.

"That's it, kitten." Malcolm's voice causes my eyes to crack open. "Come on my fingers like the good girl you are."

Well, hell. When he puts it that way...

I shatter. My moan is breathy, and Malcolm tsks softly in my ear.

"I think we can do better than that, don't you?" His tongue snakes out to lave my ear, causing me to shiver with the aftershocks of my orgasm. "We aren't finished here until you're screaming my name."

Sounds like a plan to me!

Malcolm's mouth starts to move its way down my body, gently nipping and licking a path right to my core. I can practically feel my ovaries sit up and cheer when his face is finally between my legs.

I kind of want a picture of him down there. It's a damn good look for him.

Pussy tamer. I can't fight the twitch of my lips at the thought.

Malcolm isn't paying attention to my face. Instead, his gaze is fixed on my pussy, his eyes dark with desire. He blows out a breath that has my legs shaking. I had no idea I could be this sensitive.

I'd always enjoyed sex in the past, most shifters did, but having sex with your mate is out of this world. I chalked it up to the stupid expressions mates got whenever they so much as thought about one another, but now, having experienced it for myself, I can see what all the fuss is really about.

The brush of Malcolm's tongue against my clit breaks me out of my mate musings and slams me back to the present. The pussy tamer is about to get to work, and I don't want to miss even an instant of it.

"Do you know what you taste like?" His lips are so close to my clit that they brush against it as he speaks.

Did he ask me a question?

A long, slow lick along my slit has my breath leaving me in a huff, but it's nothing compared to the feeling of his tongue sliding into my pussy and lapping me up like a damn kitten with milk.

My legs start to shake, and Malcolm pulls back, slowly licking his lips as he does. "You taste like the smoothest, sweetest honey with just a tiny kick that makes me crave more." He leans in to lick me again. "And I'll never get enough."

My brain can't seem to form words as I watch him dive back between my legs. He's not eating me out. That's too nice of a phrase. He is *attacking* my pussy with his mouth. His magic lashes against my nipples, and I feel my eyes roll into the back of my head.

Are you going to come all over my tongue? Once you have, I'll have you coming all over my dick. His dark rumblings have my pussy clenching as I draw closer to the edge of oblivion. *That's it, kitten. Come for me again.*

Oh fuck. Stars burst behind my eyelids as I come, chanting Malcolm's name to the heavens.

My body is still shaking from my second orgasm when Malcolm lifts me. In a blink, we're no longer in my room, and he's bending me over the war room table.

"Lift your leg onto the table kitten." His gruff order has me shivering and panting as I comply.

His hands caress my hips, his teeth nipping at the mate mark on my neck. My head drops forward, and I arch my ass against his hips as I moan his name. I need him to fill me. Right. Now.

"How badly do you want my cock buried in your pretty little pussy, kitten?"

Who the hell knew Malcolm was such a dirty talker? I'm kind of living for it.

I whimper, but I know from the bond that he won't give me what I want until I answer him. "I want it more than I want my next breath."

"Will you clean it off once I'm finished with you?"

At this point he could ask anything of me and I'd give it to him if he would just put his damn dick inside me. I can feel him chuckle down the bond as he picks up on my thoughts. My mental walls are completely down right now, and I don't care if he's reading my mind.

"Soon, I'm going to have you choking on my cock." Holy. Fuck.

Chapter Eight

I don't have more time to process his statement before Malcolm slams his cock into me. My pussy contracts around him, and I drop my forehead onto the table.

"I love how wet you get for me, kitten." I can hear the smug smirk on his face as he continues to pound into me. "You're so hot and tight. It's like your pussy never wants to let me go."

Probably because she doesn't ever want to let him go. Not when it feels this good.

His magic lashes against my clit, and I can feel my channel begin to convulse around his cock. He presses a hand against my upper back, pulling my hips more firmly against his at the same time, causing him to slide deeper.

"Right there!" I cry as he picks up the pace. "Yes! Malcolm, yes!"

"Scream my name when you come, kitten. I want this whole damn house to know I'm fucking this pussy."

I hadn't realized that dirty talk could make me come. But hey, you live and you learn.

My scream echoes off the walls as I clench so hard around

Malcolm's cock I'm afraid I'm going to somehow cut it off. Malcolm's answering roar sends another mini orgasm barreling through me. He can't move much because my pussy has a death grip on his dick, but that doesn't seem to bother him any.

My last thought before I black out is that the man has mad cock game.

~

DESPITE WAKING up in the middle of the night and staying awake for a few hours after, I feel damn good. Great sex does that for you.

I'm pulling on a baggy sweater and some leggings, opting for comfort over fashion today, when I feel a grin spread across my face—for the tenth time since Malcolm and I tore ourselves from my bed. We showered quickly and he ran to get himself dressed. When we're finished, we'll meet the rest of the group back in the war room.

I swiftly braid my hair and head out into the hall, that stupid grin returning when I spy my mate leaning against the wall opposite my door. My panther stretches and purrs, letting it rumble through my chest. Malcolm's eyes narrow on my chest, and the smile he gives me makes me want to drag him back into my room.

Mates shouldn't have to leave their room for at least a year after finalizing the bond. It should be law.

"I take it she's happy." His hand rests against my lower back, causing my panther to preen.

"Very much so."

His hand drops to my ass, and I can't help rolling my eyes. Men.

Fayden is the only person in the war room when we enter. I glance to the spot Malcolm bent me over before looking at her. She's typing away furiously on a tablet, her brows furrowed. Uh-oh. Something isn't right.

"Hey, Fay. What's wrong?" Malcolm moves away from me and heads over to his sister. "What's happening?"

"I..." Fayden looks from Malcolm to me, appearing lost. "I have no idea what's going on. The program..." Her voice fades as she gestures to the tablet.

I pull up a seat next to Fayden and gently place my hand on her arm. "It's okay. Everything we've been through is new. We may just need to tweak the magic a bit. We won't know for sure until you tell us what's happening."

"I'm only getting snap shots and images of the future. Nothing that will really help." Frustration flashes in her eyes. "This has never happened before."

"Have you ever dealt with gods before?" When she shakes her head, I smile. "There we go. I'm sure this is going to help us, especially with locating Ayla's sisters, but it might not be too helpful when it comes to the rest. We're really in uncharted territory."

"She's right," Ayla calls from the door, causing all of us to look over at her. There's something different about her today. I can't tell what it is, but she's glowing. "I think a lot of the answers we need have been lost with time. Otherwise, I would have some inkling of what the hell is going on, especially now that I have my memories back."

Caleb comes in behind her, appearing a little more puffed up and protective than normal. My eyes instantly narrow on my best friend. Something is up. I'm going to have to attack her once we're alone again.

"That makes sense," Fayden responds. "If we don't have the information we need for the data to accurately form a prediction..." She trails off and starts frantically tapping on her tablet again.

Ayla stops abruptly, her eyes shooting between Malcolm

and me, and a sly grin spreads across her face. Caleb seems just as smug, but quietly hands Ayla some money.

My jaw drops. "Did you two *bet* on us?"

Malcolm's focus shifts to our friends, a scowl on his face.

"We all know you're mates. I said you'd get him to plunder your treasure chest sooner than Caleb."

My eyes narrow further.

Caleb's shoulders shake with laughter when he says, "I figured Malcolm would wait at least another week before claiming you."

My eyes drift back to the spot on the table where not so long ago I was getting railed by the male now standing behind me. My mate.

I can feel you getting wet, kitten, he purrs, and I clench my thighs. *Santa Mierda.*

You are a dirty, dirty witch. He chuckles softly at my accusation.

We're so wrapped up in each other, we miss anything else Ayla and Caleb say about our mating. Fayden giggles lightly.

"I'm going to call Kelly and Darcy. I want you to play us those images, Fayden." Caleb brings up a screen to video chat with our group back home.

Kelly's face appears on the screen, and she gestures for us to hold on before disappearing from sight, presumably to go get the others. Soon, Connor, Dante, Darcy, and Xin have crowded into Kelly's office with her.

"Hi, everyone!" Kelly's voice is as soothing and calming as ever. I hadn't realized just how much I've missed her until this very moment. Once we got all the answers we could here, we needed to make sure the gang was reunited as quickly as possible.

"Has everything been quiet on the home front?" Ayla asks.

"Thankfully, yes," Xin answers. "Everyone is settling in

well, and we haven't heard a peep from any demons."

"They seem to have followed us across the pond," I state with a sigh. "I suppose it was too much to hope that Malick would fuck off for a while longer."

"We heard about the fight," Kelly comments, her eyes trailing along my body in a way that tells me she's making sure I'm not still injured. Aw, I love that bitch.

"We wanted to see if you'd been able to dig anything up in your research. We also want to show you what Malcolm's sister has been working on." I smile at Kelly reassuringly.

"It looks like what we know, or what we've seen, comes from multiple religious factions. We assumed this to be the case, but getting confirmation from you has helped us narrow things down to what might actually be true." Connor has a tablet in front of him. "A lot about our origins has been lost to time. Thankfully, with Darcy here, we've been able to get a sense of what happened during those early days."

Darcy nods, her eyes dimming slightly. "A lot of what I remember is hazy from that time. There was so much fighting and chaos. I have a sneaking suspicion that the gods removed most of my knowledge, and any other original's knowledge, of that time."

"Which suggests," Connor inserts, "that Darcy and the other originals knew something about these Härja. They had the information at one time, but the gods had deemed that knowledge too dangerous. It's odd that Darcy can remember her creation, both as a witch and a vampire, but the term Härja and the images she saw with you guys are foreign to her.

"We know shifters and witches were the first creations of the gods, and humans came about later, so it stands to reason that we had some part to play in the war you witnessed. It's possible we were created as some form of soldier. Since witches and shifters breed so fast, we could have, in theory, overwhelmed the Härja with sheer numbers sooner or later, especially since neither the gods nor the Härja seem to have been able to reproduce."

Out of the corner of my eye, I see Fayden tapping away on her tablet, entering in all of this information in the hopes of getting a better prediction from her creation.

"Can we start at the beginning and piece information in?" Fayden's voice is more confident now than it had been when I first walked into the room. Good. "I want to make sure I have all the relevant data in my system before we show you what I've been working on, Uncle Connor."

Ayla coughs a laugh into her hand. Quiet, nerdy Connor was Uncle Connor. It was kind of adorable. My lips twitch when I catch Kelly giving Connor the gooey eyes of someone who is staring at a particularly adorable puppy, but Connor just ignores the look and nods at Fayden.

"You're right, Fay. I forgot about your project. Let me send you all of the data we have." He turns to look at Darcy. "You put everything you remember in here, right?" At her nod, Connor taps on his tablet, and the telltale *whoosh* sound of a sent email tells us we now have what they have.

"Thanks, Uncle Connor! It'll take me a bit to download and input the data," she says in a distracted tone. Her eyes dance over the screen, her fingers following suit. "But I still want to show everyone the isolated images I was able to get."

Everybody nods and moves a bit closer. The anticipation is palpable, and I can feel my panther pacing restlessly, itching for more information so she can act.

Calm down, I soothe. *We can't be all riled up. I won't be able to focus.*

Something isn't right, she rumbles in reply.

How so?

The other day, you said it felt as though we are all pawns. That's true, and I still feel that way. *If the gods truly believe in free will,*

*why not give us the information we need to make whatever moves we
have to in order to keep everyone safe?*

I... Mierda. She has a point. Giving us more information
would help us make more informed decisions without
tampering with our free will. My heart plummets at the
thought.

"What if the gods don't even really know what's
happening?"

"Or," Ayla murmurs, "what if they don't have the power
they once had?"

That notion sends ice shooting through every nerve in my
body.

"We saw them struggling against *seven*," Ayla continues.
"There were hundreds of them against seven. They couldn't
destroy those beings, instead they locked them away. At least
that's what I gathered from what we saw."

"If they couldn't end them, how are we supposed to?" I
question, my voice trembling.

"One thing at a time," Kelly soothes. "Let's gain more
information. We may not even need to destroy the Härja. We
may only need to permanently seal them away."

"That's a far more manageable task," Darcy agrees.

I shake myself out of my gloomy thoughts and nod. They
are right. Focus on what we can do instead of what seems like
an impossible task.

I CAN ONLY STARE at the images on the screen, my mouth
slightly ajar. The shock from the others pulses through the
war room.

Malick is bent over a painfully stunning woman, his hand
resting almost lovingly on her cheek.

The massive Härja we saw in the past has his fingers

wrapped around my throat. Both of us are covered in blood, and Ayla's lifeless body is at his feet.

Two cloaked figures stand beside an archdemon who looks disturbingly like Malick, but isn't, as he looms over Kelly who is surrounded by demons, their essence draining into her glowing body.

Darcy, covered in blood, is lost in the throes of bloodlust.

Another woman, one who looks a lot like Ayla, is laid out on a stone slab with a spear sticking out of her chest.

Shaken, I turn to look at those around me, noticing everyone is just as pale and frightened as I am. It isn't until that moment that I fully comprehend that everyone I love could very possibly die on this little quest. I knew it. But being hit in the face with it is something else entirely, and it feels as though my soul is being stripped from my body one painful piece at a time.

"How accurate is this thing again?" Malcolm mutters to his sister.

"Prior to this, it had been almost ninety-eight percent accurate. But it also showed video, not images. I can't honestly say how accurate this is." Fayden chews on her lip, looking uncertain.

Another image flashes before us. It's of me, holding a box with the Celtic knot symbol that had been on the mantel at the cottage. I stiffen. That box!

"Stop!" My hand goes flying out. "I pulled that box out from under a bed in the cottage before we were attacked!" My eyes fly to Malcolm. "That's what was bothering me last night!" My gaze swings to Ayla and Caleb. "Did anyone grab it from the cottage after the battle?"

Ayla shakes her head, shooting a glance at Caleb for confirmation. "We didn't go back into the cottage and haven't been back since. I didn't even know about the box until just now. You called me into the room when we were attacked."

"Is it safe to go back?" I ask.

Malcolm and Caleb share a look before they both nod. "We've had the cottage watched and there hasn't been any sign of demonic activity."

"And that's it for the images. I couldn't see what was in the box, just Olivia holding it." Fayden, her tone distracted, has her nose buried in her tablet.

I stand, and Malcolm moves to place a protective hand on my lower back. He leans over and disconnects the call with the rest of our community before leading us out of the war room. I can feel the tension radiating out of his body as we continue out of the castle.

What's wrong? I wrap my arm around him, my fingers finding a small swatch of skin between his shirt and pants.

I'm remembering the last time you were at the cottage.

Hey. I'm okay. We can't avoid battles.

I know. He sighs. *I know. But it doesn't make this any easier. You're my mate, Liv. The fact that I wasn't there when you needed it...*His magic swirls in vicious lashes around him. *I won't fail you as a mate again.*

We'll come back to that when we're not about to go open a random magical box. But you didn't fail me, Malcolm.

He doesn't respond, instead he opens a portal to the cottage. I let him drop the subject for the time being, but we'll need to talk about it eventually.

It's ingrained in mates to want to take care of and protect each other, so I can understand why he feels the way he does. However, we're not exactly in normal circumstances.

The area around the cottage is quiet and peaceful, the wind whipping against the cliffs providing the only sound. It's soothing, especially after what happened the last time I was here. I don't sense any taint left behind by the demons, and the wards around the cottage are still holding strong.

Here goes nothing.

Chapter Nine

The cottage is, surprisingly, exactly as we left it. For some reason, I assumed the inside would be as chaotic as I felt, a physical reflection of my own turmoil. Silly, I now realize, but seeing it still pristine seems wrong. It's hard to believe only a few days have passed.

My heart rate picks up, and I force myself to take a few deep, calming breaths. I've never had a panic attack before, and I don't think that's what this is. Whatever is going on, it feels like I'm having heart failure.

A soothing brush down the mate bond has me settling and relaxing. Malcolm's hand squeezes mine, and the remnants of doubt leave me. Ayla and I aren't alone. Our mates are here, and so are quite a few enforcers from the Council. We're safe.

The box is still sitting on the bed where I left it, looking completely innocuous, but we all know there is nothing innocent about that box. Regardless of what's inside, it is tied to this twisted path we are being forced to walk.

We grew up with the understanding that the gods were

the good guys. After everything we've been through, all without the insight and knowledge the gods have, I am beginning to question that. Morally gray? Possibly. Overall good guys? Definitely not. They are admittedly better than the Härja, but as of right now, not by much.

Ayla makes her way over to the bed, staring intently at the box before turning to look at me.

"Together?"

I nod. "Together."

I move to stand next to her, while Caleb and Malcolm stand protectively by the door. My fingers tremble slightly as I reach out for the box. I hold it between the two of us, and Ayla reaches for the top, her fingers also shaking. Gently, almost as though she's afraid something is going to shoot out of the box and attack us, Ayla removes the lid.

And nothing happens.

It's a bit anticlimactic.

We peer inside. There are six charms, etched with the symbol from the mantle and box, and a piece of parchment sealed with wax.

"My mother's seal," Ayla whispers as she stares at the contents of the box.

Caleb and Malcolm move to join us, looking into the box as well.

"I was expecting...more," Malcolm murmurs, his brows arched. "Considering everything we've experienced throughout this whole adventure, I thought there'd be something in there that would, I don't know, eat us? Melt the skin off our bones? Boil our eyes out of our head?"

Dios Mío. What the ever loving fuck is wrong with him? I turn to look at Malcolm, my own brows raised. I run my eyes over him, inspecting him as one might a deranged serial killer.

"What the hell is wrong with you?" My voice conveys that I think he needs to be locked in a small padded room for our safety. "Boil our eyes out of our heads?" I shake my head.

"What?" He shoots me an innocent look. "Given everything, it doesn't seem like a stretch."

Caleb's shoulders shake as he tries to suppress his laughter, and Ayla just stares at Malcolm like he's been possessed—which is entirely possible. Malcolm glances at the three of us, holding up his hands, palms out, in defense.

"It doesn't!"

If I didn't still have the box in my hands, I would facepalm myself so hard I'd probably knock myself out.

Why the hell are men so weird? I shoot the question to Ayla.

That inquiry seems to set her off, and she launches into a fit of giggles. This starts a chain reaction and has Caleb chuckling along with her. My lips start twitching, but I'm determined not to laugh.

Malcolm's eyes light with glee as he starts chuckling along with them. I roll my eyes and place the box back on the bed, still fighting to keep my own laughter in check. I wrap my fingers around the parchment. I have a feeling the charms are for the women in our group, but I don't want to play with them just yet.

Ayla steps closer and looks over my shoulder, nodding for me to open the seal and read what's inside. I break the wax and carefully uncurl the paper. It doesn't feel brittle, like one would expect of something that's a few hundred years old. Instead, it feels as though the parchment was just recently placed in the box. I'm slightly surprised to find that the ink is completely dry.

My dearest daughter,

The fact that you are reading this letter means I have failed, and you must face a threat so great I fear none will survive.

I have done all I can to ensure you have the tools and friends you need when the time comes—the seer's daughter, the sin eater, the original, your sisters, your mates, your allies. I have done all I can to guarantee they find their way to you, as the goddess wished it so.

I cannot, however, prepare for everything, my daughter. And so, I must caution you to be selective in those you trust. The road before you is far more dangerous than the one you've previously traveled. I am unable to provide all the answers, as so much has been lost to time, just as the gods willed it. I fear even they have forgotten the full extent of the events that are unfolding.

The location of your sisters rests with the seer's daughter. I have wiped the memory of those precise locations from everyone, even myself, to keep them safe. While I had planned to hide you too, I always knew you would be the one to walk this world awake and alone. My soul aches to think of you without your memories, always on the run, but you have your family and your mate now.

My sweet daughter, you and your sisters are the Fates—seals to the gates of Hell, special guardians that keep the balance in check. You and your sisters hold back a plague that, should it be released, would ravage this world until all are either dead or enslaved. You were given this terrible gift the night you three were born, hand selected by the goddess Brigid. I hoped to spare you from what's to come, to push the prophecy off until the next generation of Fates, but I suppose you cannot outrun your destiny.

I will give you one small spark of hope to cling to during the darkness that is to come. Fight for the tiny spark of life that lives within you, for the life created during the darkest of times shines the brightest and purest of all.

The prophecy will only get you part of the way. Believe in your community. Believe in yourself.

I love you so much, my beautiful, strong daughter.

Three Fates pure to keep the gate,

past, present, future.
Should one Fate fall the seals will break,
maiden, mother, crone.
Two Fates more shall fall, and Hell shall wake,
life, death, rebirth.
New queens will rise to fight for light,
female, queen, goddess.
A sacrifice will heal the breach,
shifter, witch, vampire.
Three new Fates will be the key.

Love,
Your mother.

~

THE SILENCE that filters in around us is almost uncomfortable and has me twitching to break it. There is a lot in that letter that has to be unraveled, but we're going to need the rest of the group to do that.

"I think," Caleb starts, "we need to head back to the war room. We'll need to give this to Fayden and call the others again."

I nod absentmindedly as I replay what the letter said. *I'm the seer's daughter, but I have no freaking clue where the hell Ayla's sisters are.* The memory from the other day comes to mind. I'd seen Ayla's mother come to mine for help. I'm only a few years older than Ayla and her sisters which is why I hadn't realized any of this before now.

Mama might have some insight, my panther responds. She's right, but she wouldn't be happy with just a call, she'd insist on a visit. I groan internally. A visit with the family meant a trip to Mexico and a huge headache.

Maybe I can get Mama to give me answers over the phone... if I beg.

My panther snorts, knowing full well that will never happen. Mama can be difficult, and it's been a long time since I visited.

"Liv?"

"Huh, what?" I look around, trying to determine who called my name. "Sorry, what?"

"I asked if you were ready to head back?" Ayla murmurs as she studies my face. "You okay?"

"Yeah..." I force a smile. "Yeah, let's go."

BACK IN THE WAR ROOM, Fayden already inputs the information from the letter while I start pacing. There is a lot to unpack in that missive, and once again, it leaves us with more questions than answers.

I tug on the end of my braid as the others call the New England team, their faces all popping up. They all appear eager to learn what we found, but I have a feeling I'm not the only one who will be put in the spotlight without any answers to give. It's going to be a long day.

We recap the contents of the letter and show the others the charms that were in the box, and an unsettling silence falls over our group as we all retreat into our thoughts.

I can't take it anymore. "I'm the seer's daughter."

All eyes turn to me and hold. So this is what any sort of specimen being studied feels like. Not so great.

"My mother is a seer."

"Hold the phone," Ayla says. "Since when is Ximena a Seer?"

I can't fight the eye roll. "She's *always* been a seer. She doesn't advertise it because it takes a lot out of her, and she doesn't like knowing how her loved ones die."

It's a sobering thought.

Seers are rare and can come from any species. There are always limitations on what a seer can see, including how far into the future their visions take them and whether or not that future can change. Mama is pretty damn accurate. I don't know of any instances when her visions were wrong or able to be changed. They always drained her pretty severely, and if she called on a vision instead of allowing one to come naturally, she typically didn't have another for at least a week. I think the longest was a month.

"Mama Mena is a seer." Ayla sounds like she's getting used to the idea. "Is *Abuela* anything special?"

"I mean the woman took on the conquistadors, so that makes her pretty damn special," I reply with a grin.

"Valid point," she concedes. "Okay. So you're the seer's daughter. We know Darcy is the original. Who the hell is the sin eater?" She starts pacing, and I resume my strides right alongside her.

"Just based on logic alone," Fayden interjects, "it's Kelly." She hasn't raised her head from her tablet, but her words land like a bomb.

Kelly's face drains of color, and for a second, she appears completely, utterly lost. I wish she was here so I could hug the crap out of her. Clearly, she has no idea what she really is if this is true.

"There's no way." The denial in her statement is strong, and she's shaking her head. "No way. I've never been able to do anything a sin eater can do."

"I'm not so sure of that..." Ayla's voice rips my attention away from Kelly. "The first time I met you, I noticed some of your power was locked away. I thought you knew."

Sin eaters, like queens, were the things of legend. They'd

been hunted just as fiercely as the queens because of their ability to decimate demons with a thought. Depending on how powerful one was, they could kill a legion in seconds. If Kelly is a Sin Eater... The possibilities were endless.

"I need to talk to my mother." Kelly ended the call, and we were left in yet another awkward silence.

Chapter Ten

"If you knew where my sisters are, you would have said something by now," Ayla says, cutting through the silence. "Do you think it's something like what happened to me?"

I shrug. To be honest, my mother didn't have the magic to take my memories, and we'd lived pretty secluded lives, even when the family had been primarily located in the States, so I don't think my mother hired a witch.

This was so frustrating. I tug on my braid in annoyance.

"I don't think so," I mumble.

Malcolm comes over and wraps his arms around me, pulling me in close to his chest. "We'll figure this out. Want to call your mom?"

Ayla starts to cackle.

"No." I sigh. "My mother won't answer questions about something like this over the phone. We're going to have to go to Mexico."

Ayla cackles louder, so I shoot her a dirty look.

"This isn't funny."

"It really is though. Malcolm is going to meet both Mena

and *Abuela*. This is going to be great!" She wipes tears from her eyes. "They're going to kill you."

I feel Malcolm stiffen behind me. That scene from *The Lego Movie* comes to mind, where Batman just goes "Ugghhh-hhh," and it plays on an endless loop. While I'm busy internally dying, Malcolm has gone from rigid to chuckling, his chest rumbling against my back.

"I look forward to the challenge of getting them to like me."

Cue the continuation of that endless loop. They didn't *like* anyone. They were crotchety old women who took great pleasure in making you feel so awkward and squirm so much that you just up and died without thought.

"They're going to *love* you!" Ayla laughs. That traitor.

I cough and clear my throat. "Right. They are insane. Just know they're insane. They might try to kill all of us in our sleep."

"Sounds like fun," is his response.

"I didn't realize you were a masochist." I spin in his arms to glare up at him. He chuckles in response, leaning down to press a light kiss to my lips.

"Don't worry, kitten. Everything will be fine."

"Your funeral."

I pull away from him, fishing my phone out of my pocket. I might as well get this over with and rip the Band-Aid off. I stare at my phone for a minute before wincing as I press the dial button.

She answers on the first ring.

"Mija!" She sounds pleased and irritated at the same time. Ah, the steaming side dish of guilt is about to be served. "You haven't called me in almost a year!" She proceeds to cuss me out in a stream of Spanish so rapid that even I have trouble keeping up.

I hit the speakerphone button as I roll my eyes. It's best

to just let her tire herself out. Malcolm casts an amused glance at the phone, and Ayla and Caleb meander over to be part of the conversation.

There's a soft thud on the other end, and my *abuela's* voice comes over the line. "Mena," she chides my mother, "you let Olivia speak. She has called for a reason. You can reprimand her later."

Bless her.

"Fine, Mama, but she should be more considerate of her poor mama. Being so far away... she should call more." I just want to slam my head against the wall. It's the same conversation over and over again.

"Mama," I insert, "*Abuela* is right. There is a reason I called. I'm sorry I haven't called before now, I will explain later."

She scoffs. "Later? *Later*, she says." She's ramping herself up for another tangent, but before she starts, I cut her off.

"Mama," I scold. "We're coming for a visit." That kills any angry ranting she was about to unleash on me. "We have a lot to discuss, Mama, and I know you'll want to tell us this story in person."

There's a pregnant pause on the other end before another thud sounds. "Ximena, what have I told you. You should have told her sooner."

So they know why we're coming. My *abuela* was always astute.

"*Sí, mija*, I'll want to tell you this in person." My mother sounds more subdued than I've ever heard her. "When will you be here?"

"Later today. We're portaling in."

"I'll prepare rooms. *Mija*..." She takes a deep breath before continuing. "I knew this day was coming. I couldn't tell you before now, but it's a relief to be able to talk about it."

That surprises me. My mother isn't usually one for apologies...or guilt. This tells me she hadn't withheld anything from me out of a need to protect me, she'd done it because she had no other choice.

"There's one more thing, Mama." I don't want to warn them before showing up, but after that, I feel like I need to. "My mate is coming with me."

Abuela starts to cackle in glee on the other end of the phone. A smile laces my mother's voice when she says, "Good. You've found him. Tell him we have the perfect plot of land picked out for his final resting place."

"Mama..." I warn. The line goes dead with both of those devil women laughing.

"So that went well." Ayla snickers.

I shrug. "About as well as can be expected considering she's the devil." This gets a laugh out of Ayla and Caleb, and an amused smile from Malcolm. "Just be warned, they are both evil."

THE PORTAL before me leads to some of Mexico's dense rainforest. My ancestors were Aztec, and they lived in these jungles alongside humans until the conquistadors showed up. My *abuela* fought alongside her human neighbors, but there were too many of them. She eventually fled to the States with my mother and the rest of our clan.

Now, centuries later, they were finally back in our ancestral home.

I inhale a deep breath as I step through the portal. *Home*. My panther and I are comforted by the scents and sounds of the jungle around us. I want to shift and run through the trees, and feel the rough bark dig into my paws before giving way beneath my razor-sharp claws.

That will have to wait until after we sit down with my

family though. That Batman scene is looping through my head again.

Malcolm steps forward and takes my hand, lacing his fingers through mine and squeezing gently. I squeeze back, finding immense comfort in his presence.

A large male panther prowls close to us, quickly shifting into a familiar form. Caleb lets out a low growl at the sight of the naked male, and I can practically hear Ayla rolling her eyes. Malcolm slaps a hand over my eyes, his own growl rumbling out of him. He isn't a shifter, but he sure can growl like one. It is fucking hot.

"Hi, Diego." The laughter in my voice has Malcolm stiffening next to me. "Everyone, meet my cousin Diego."

"*Hola!*" He sounds exactly the same as the last time I saw him, which is a silly thought to have, but it warms my heart anyway. Just another piece of home. "I've come to show you to the village."

"You can do that as a panther," Malcolm deadpans.

"I suggest you shift," Caleb threatens.

I bite my lip to keep myself from laughing. I can feel Ayla's similar struggle through the pack bond.

"You guys could just pee a circle around us, ya know." There's a small part of me that finds Malcolm's territorial behavior appealing, but the majority of me snaps her fingers and reminds that small part I'm a strong, independent woman who doesn't need no man.

"That might get the message across quicker," Ayla agrees. "Should we get a sign and tape it to our foreheads? Property of a grouchy alpha male?"

"Watch it," Caleb murmurs.

Malcolm pulls his hand away from my face, and I can see Diego has shifted back. But I also notice Malcolm is holding two small stickers in his hand. *He didn't.* I look up into his eyes and see the laughter sparkling there.

"Here." He hands one to me and one to Ayla. Mine reads "Property of Malcolm, Lord of Witches, he who has the biggest dick, tamer of pussies, and all-around general badass."

"Are you serious right now?" My brows shoot up to my hairline. "The *only* pussy you're taming is mine." My panther growls in agreement. "Ayla, what does yours say?"

"Property of Caleb, Lord of the Dragon Pussy, noble steed, spitter of shit, and all-around general douche bag." She laughs as she reads hers allowed. Caleb's growl replaces mine, and I can't fight the giggle that bursts from my lips.

"Payback is going to be so, so sweet, you dumb fuck."

"Onward, noble steed!" Malcolm cries with one of his hands thrust into the sky. Caleb steps up behind him and punches him in the side.

He looks to me while Malcolm clutches his ribs. "I want it noted I did not dick punch him out of respect for you."

"So it is noted," I state in a somber tone.

With that, we all turn to follow Diego into the jungle.

AFTER ABOUT FORTY-FIVE minutes of walking, we finally make it to my mother's village. Built within the trees of the jungle, the huts are small and adorable. They live simply here.

A small boy runs up holding a pair of shorts. Diego shifts and pulls them on, then he ruffles the boy's hair in thanks. "This is my son, Beto."

"I didn't know Maria was pregnant! Why didn't anyone tell me! He looks so big!" I squat down with a smile. "*Hola*, I'm your cousin Olivia."

Beto sticks his thumb in his mouth and waves a tiny hand.

"He's three. We've kept it pretty hush-hush. Aunty Mena

knew what was coming for you, and she didn't want to run the risk of not having you where you were meant to be." He shrugs. "Once all of this is done, we know you'll come visit as often as you want. Especially since you're shacking up with a witch."

"True." I stand and look around the village. Bridges span the distance between the trees. On the forest floor, there's a large communal fire, several tents where food is prepared and eaten, and a small hut for visitors who aren't comfortable sleeping in the trees. "Speaking of Satan...where is she?"

Diego chuckled and gestured above him. "She's at home, waiting for you."

"Like the creep she is." He chuckled again. "I'll see you around, Diego."

"Good luck!"

We need it.

We make our way up to the village in the trees. Each step closer to my mother has me wanting to walk in the other direction. I honestly shouldn't complain. She's a wonderful, loving mother, but she's a menace.

We're not even at her door when she comes bursting out, waving her hands in the air as she spots us. *"Mija!"*

Despite all my earlier grumblings, I open my arms and rush to hug her. She may be a pain in the ass, but she feels like home, damn it.

"Mama."

"Mija." She squeezes me in her arms. "I have missed you so much."

"I've missed you too, Mama."

"We will get you sorted, *mija*. I promise." She holds me out at arm's length to study me before her gaze travels over my shoulder to my companions.

"Now which one is the mate?"

I groan softly. "Mama, you don't need to interrogate him."

"Nonsense. I would never do such a thing."

I snort. "Okay."

Malcolm steps up behind me. "I'm Malcolm, Liv's mate."

My mother pushes me to the side so she can study Malcolm. Her eyes travel all over him, and she makes small noises under her breath as she does. I roll my eyes behind her back, and Malcom's eyes glitter with laughter. He's being a trooper.

"He's a witch, *mija*."

"*Sí*, Mama."

"I don't know, *mija*."

"It's too late for that, Mama. The bond has already been finalized."

"I suppose he'll do then." With that, she spins to go back into her house.

Malcolm's shoulders tremble with laughter, and he shakes his head as he follows me into my mother's home. Caleb and Ayla are right behind us.

Despite how small the space actually is, the wall of windows at the back makes it feel so much bigger. The hut has a small loft where my mother sleeps, and the downstairs is an open concept living room with an eat-in kitchen. I take a deep breath and let the scent of home wash over me.

New England will always be where I'm meant to be. My adult home. But here...this is far more comforting than I thought it would be. I could, I suppose, admit that I needed my mother's help more than I thought.

"Take a seat." My mother gestures around the living room and goes into the kitchen to grab some water for everyone. As she comes back, she says, "*Abuela* will be here soon, and we can start. She'll have some pieces of her own to add."

We converse as we wait for my grandmother. She doesn't live far, but she lives by the philosophy that she never arrives late, everyone else is simply early, à la *The Princess Diaries*.

The door opens and my *abuela*, all five feet of her, fills the room. She's tiny but has more personality in her little toe than most people have in their whole body. My mother is the spitting image of her, so I know exactly what Mama will look like when she's older than dirt. My mother looks to be in her late thirties or early forties, while *Abuela* appears to be in her early sixties. Shifters age well.

"Nieta!" Abuela's grin causes one to stretch across my face. "I am so happy you are here." Her eyes go to Malcolm and narrow. "Is this *el compañero?*"

"Sí, abuela. This is my mate." I grab hold of Malcolm's hand. "This is Malcolm."

She sniffs and lifts her nose into the air. "He's a witch."

"Don't you start, *abuela.* I seem to recall some interesting stories of your dalliances from your youth." My grin turns predatory. "Didn't you seduce Cortez?"

"The Cortez?" Malcolm asks.

Abuela hair flips like the best of them and scoffs. "Of course *the* Cortez. How else was I supposed to get information on where he would attack next? When I got tired of him, we fought. He's lucky his guards showed up, or he would have died a lot sooner than he did."

So my *abuela* may be a bit of a badass. She fucked *and* fought Cortez.

"I'll allow it," *Abuela* announces as she glances between Malcolm and me.

I roll my eyes for what feels like the millionth time today. She'll allow it... Yeah, okay.

"Thank you, *Abuela.*" I'm not sure I'm completely successful at keeping the sarcasm out of my tone. "That's very generous of you."

Ayla snorts around a laugh. It's the first sound she's made since we entered my mother's house. Apparently my mother scares her too.

"Olivia has come here for a purpose, Mama," my mother chastises *Abuela,* as though she didn't just do something similar. These two, I swear. "And we don't have much time. There's so much to tell, and I'm sure they'll have a lot of questions."

"Sí," Abuela sighs as she sits next to my mother. They both look grim now. That's a great sign.

Chapter Eleven

According to my mother, Aine had come to her soon after the Goddess Brigid told her that her daughters were selected to be the next Fates. Aine wanted to know what the future held for her children. She'd gotten wind of the prophecy and was worried—rightfully so—that it was about her girls.

Mama confirmed that the prophecy was indeed about her daughters, though she didn't know where the prophecy had originated from. Devastated, Aine left, apparently determined to come up with a plan to save her children. My mother hadn't just confirmed the prophecy, she'd also told Aine her daughters' lives were in peril. My mother couldn't see the entity that wanted her girls, but she knew it was darker and more powerful than anything she'd ever felt before.

Aine came back a year later to once again ask my mother about her daughters' future. This time, though, she made plans to protect them. She wanted to know if what she had done was enough to keep them alive.

My mother can't always see on demand, but with Aine and

her daughters, she was able to call visions at will. Mama assumed it was the will of the gods and didn't question it. My memory rushed back to me at this part. She'd been able to confirm that her daughters would be safe where they were hidden. She'd also confirmed that they would have until the triplets were roughly one hundred years old to ensure the spots they selected were secure before demons came for them, but she couldn't tell Aine an exact date.

"Is that why she wrote I know where Sorcha and Isobel are?" I ask, interrupting my mother's story.

She shot me a glare that made me wince. "*Sí*. Because you heard us as we talked about it in more detail, but considering how young you were, I'm not surprised you don't remember."

"This is where I come in. I recorded everything in this." *Abuela* hands me a leather-bound journal. "It's everything we knew, including all the coordinates and information on the traps that were set,.."

Staring at the journal, I don't immediately reach for it. They knew about the prophecy all this time. They knew I had a part to play in all of this, yet they never told me.

Was this how Ayla felt when she learned her mother had taken her memories?

A little betrayed? Hurt? Confused? Scared?

This is all starting to feel like too much.

Needing air, I shoot to my feet and fly out the door, walking away from my mother's house as quickly as I can. There's a small part of me that feels childish for leaving, but I just need a moment to myself.

Malcolm was right, there has been a lot of change lately. I thought I'd been processing it all well. I guess I've been lying to myself.

~

ABOUT AN HOUR LATER, Malcolm finds me as I sit on a branch against the trunk of a large tree not far from the village, and he settles beside me.

"How are you holding up?" His low rumble helps to settle me. So does the fact that he waited to find me.

I rest my head against his shoulder, still staring into the depths of the jungle. "I'm not sure, to be honest." I sigh, pulling on the end of my braid. "You were right when you said this is a lot to handle. I didn't need time to wait for you," I add, "but I don't think I have been properly processing any of this."

His arm slips around me, and he leans his head against mine. "I'm here to help with that. I *want* to help with that."

He presses a kiss to the top of my head, and we sit in silence for several minutes. "There's a lot riding on you ladies," he murmurs, breaking the silence, "but that doesn't mean you can't be, for lack of a better word, human. None of us can be set to 'go' all the time. We all need to turn off, recharge, and then get back to work. If you need time, we'll take time."

"But it feels like I *can't* take time," I argue. "Malcolm, it feels like time is running out. We need to find Ayla's sisters, and we need to stop the gates of Hell from opening. We need more answers."

And that's the crux of the problem. We've been running along on this fucking wild goose chase, not even one step ahead of the enemy. Hell, I'm pretty sure we're a few steps *behind* them at this point. The gods have tasked us with the impossible, and instead of giving us the tools we need to have a fighting chance, they leave us shrouded in questions that we can't seem to find a solid answer to.

To say I'm frustrated is an understatement. I'm furious. How *dare* the gods drop this at our feet. They were the ones that started it, it looks like they ran from their problems, and now they expect us to clean up after them. I want to rage, to scream. They know we won't just walk away, not with innocent lives in danger, so we're stuck between a rock and a hard place. Literally between good and evil. But the good guys aren't looking too good right about now.

"Hey." Malcom's timbre breaks me out of my raging thoughts. "I know how this makes you feel. I can feel it through our bond. I feel the same way." He presses a light kiss to my forehead. "But you aren't alone. *We* aren't alone in any of this."

"You're right." I sigh, my anger cooling. "I'm sorry I just stormed off like that. I just...I don't know. It's like my brain shut off and I needed to get out."

"No need to apologize to me. Your mother and grandmother, however..." I groan. I'm not going to live this down. "Come on," he prompts. "Let's get back to your mother's house. *Abuela* said she had more to tell us."

Yippee.

I take one last deep, cleansing breath before we head back. I have no idea how, but we're going to do this. We don't exactly have a choice.

It's eerily silent when we walk back into my mother's house. Ayla and Caleb are snuggled up together on my mother's couch. My mother and *abuela* are in the kitchen, talking in low tones. Now I feel like an ass. I scrub my hands down my face and head right for the kitchen. May as well face the music head-on.

"Oh, *mija*," my mother soothes. Her arms come around me and she hugs me close. This isn't the reaction I was expecting, but I relish the comfort she provides and sink into her embrace. "I know none of this is easy, *mija*."

My grandmother comes up behind me and places her hands on my back, offering just as much comfort as my mother. "I have more to tell you. It's all in that journal, but I want to explain."

I nod, taking one last moment to bask in the comfort of my family before pulling away.

"Go sit down with your mate. We'll be right out."

I nod again and go to settle beside Malcolm.

A few minutes later, my mother and grandmother come out of the kitchen carrying trays of food. I don't fight the small smile that spreads across my face. When in doubt, feed everyone. My mother never misses an opportunity to feed anyone she can, using literally anything as an excuse to stuff you full of delicious meals.

"Olivia," *Abuela* begins, "I told you the location of Ayla's sisters is in that journal, but there's more." Hope starts to war with dread in my stomach, and I can't make myself reach for anything my mother prepared. "Since you were so young, I took it upon myself to go in search of every scrap of information I could about the prophecy—queens, demons, the gods, everything—and it's all there in that journal."

I can feel Malcolm's awe through the bond, which mirrors my own. I don't recall a time without my *abuela* around, but I do remember her not visiting as often for a period of time. That must have been when she'd been out investigating.

"I talked with individuals who had lived with and worked beside other queens," she continues. "I'm not sure if you're aware, but our clan has never been under the guidance of a queen. We had one in the area when I was young, but we were never too involved with them, preferring to stay in the jungle and work alongside the humans that also called this area home.

"I also talked with other seers. I wanted to know what they saw in regard to this prophecy. I wasn't able to learn much through them, but what insights I did gain will help you. The origins are so murky, no one really knows how the prophecy came to be, but many of the seers I spoke to believe it has a dark origin, unlike most prophecies. They couldn't tell me why, specifically, they believed that, just that it was a feeling they all harbored.

"I also talked to those who claimed to be able to commune with the gods. Most were con artists, but there were a select few who had that rare talent. I recorded every conversation I had with them. Based on those conversations, it seemed their hands were tied with what they could do on this plane, but perhaps you'll understand more when you read those sections. I also spent quite a bit of time hunting down everything I could about the Fates."

This particularly catches my attention.

"I believe much of the information we once had was purposely lost. They have a higher purpose, something much more important than we're led to believe now, and I think the gods did this intentionally to prevent them from being harmed. Unfortunately, it means there isn't enough information to provide much guidance.

"Finally, I have chronicled our history. Not just that of shifters, but of witches, demons, and vampires. I collected as many myths, legends, and tales as I could and compiled a comprehensive timeline in an attempt to understand *why* we came to be. I feel that our origins are an important piece of this puzzle."

Shocked silence greets her when she finishes. *Santa. Mierda.* If I thought my *abuela* was badass for taking on Cortez, I was extremely wrong. I'm also tremendously touched she went to such lengths to get this information for us.

She did it because she loves us, my panther murmurs. She's been fairly quiet since we got here, which is unusual for her. But then, she's been far quieter since we gained our new powers than ever before. She was never one to talk back to me like Ayla's dragon, but she'd always been there to lend a comment or two. I just hadn't realized until now how silent she's been.

And just like that, I'm once again hit with how impossible this entire endeavor feels. I take several deep, calming breaths as I listen to the others discuss our next steps. We just gained so much valuable information, but it feels like too much to process right now.

Where the hell do we even start?

We'll start at the beginning of the journal, my panther soothes. *We can take all of this one step at a time. No need to solve everything all at once.*

I hate that my anxiety over this is impacting me so much. It's causing me to struggle when it comes to thinking rationally.

We're going to work on this together, kitten. Malcolm's voice anchors me.

Thank you.

Anything for you, kitten.

∿

LATER THAT NIGHT, we're on the jungle floor around the fire. Music is playing and people are dancing and having a good time. It's a celebration to welcome me back home. I don't feel particularly festive right now, but I'm enjoying watching my friends and family have fun.

I let the warmth of the fire sink into my bones and allow myself to just drift along the melody. I've missed this. It's not lost on me that this isn't the first time I've had this thought. Perhaps I should have spent more time here before this. It could very well be too late now.

"How's it hanging?" Ayla sits next to me, her eyes

searching my face. "Want to go blow something up with magic? Run around in your panther form? Punch someone?"

A laugh bubbles out of me. Leave it to her to be just socially awkward enough to make me feel better. "No. Not right now. But I'll let you know when the need strikes me."

Her arm slips over my shoulders in a loose hug. We were sisters before this, and everything we've experienced over the last several months has only solidified our bond. I'm lucky to have her and the others. My badass bitches.

"Why don't we take a day or two to relax here before going back with the journal?" Ayla suggests. "Decompress a bit. I'm sure your family will be thrilled to have you here for a bit longer."

"Are you sure?" Guilt hits me hard. I have the key to finding her sisters and she's offering to wait.

"They've been asleep for centuries now, another couple of days isn't going to hurt them."

I feel her reassurance through the bond. "Thank you."

"I love you, you know."

"I love you too, you crazy bitch."

Chapter Twelve

Several hours after Ayla offered to have us stay in the village for a few days, the party around us begins to die down. I'm too content to get up and head into the guest hut we've been given though, wanting to soak up as much of this as possible.

This is what I'm fighting for. My family here and my family in New England.

I feel Malcolm before I hear him. There's a slight tug on the bond that insists I look behind me and lock eyes with him. But being the contrary bitch I am, I choose to continue to stare into the fire instead.

His light footsteps get closer, and the tug on the bond becomes more persistent. Finally, I turn in my seat. My gaze locks with his heated stare. His eyes are sparkling pools of desire. Heat flows through the bond, making me squirm slightly. Flashes of images appear next—memories from our previous naked wrestling adventures and ones that haven't happened yet.

I arch a brow at him and a smirk tugs at my lips. "Can I help you with something?"

I told you I'd make you choke on my cock. My nipples harden at the reminder. *Come with me.*

I'm helpless to do anything other than obey. Need skitters down my spine and pools between my legs. *Goddess.*

He doesn't lead me far, taking me to a tree that's just outside the circle of firelight. Nerves tickle my spine next. We're in a shifter village. They'll be able to smell what we're doing and hear every noise we make. Anyone could come across us, and they won't need the light from the fire to see us either.

The thought only serves to turn me on more despite my nerves.

Malcolm leans back against the tree as I stand in front of him. His hands land on my shoulders and push me gently to my knees. I rub my palm against his jean-clad cock. He's already hard and straining against the material.

As his fingers tangle in my hair, I work to push his jeans down his legs. His cock springs free, and I bite back a moan at the sight. I grip the base and give his length a few experimental pumps, causing his hips to jerk slightly.

He pulls my face closer to his cock, a clear demand for my mouth. Feeling the need to tease him, I wrap my mouth around the head of his cock, alternating between sucking on it and swirling my tongue over the tip.

His hips arch, but I pull back and refuse to take him deeper. His hands fist in my hair, and a snarl leaves him as he holds my head steady and thrusts against my face.

It's not enough for him to hit the back of my throat. It was meant as a warning and a promise.

My lips twitch against his cock in a smirk. He told me he was going to have me choking on his cock, but he hadn't said I couldn't torture the shit out of him first.

I glide my mouth slowly down his cock, not taking nearly as much as he clearly wants me to. His ab muscles clench as I continue my slow pace, swirling my tongue around the head every time I pull back. One hand reaches down and gently cups his balls, and he lets out a low curse.

"Goddamn it, Liv." He sounds just a bit frustrated.

I make it seem as though I'm in no hurry to oblige. I feel tension coiling in him, feel him getting ready to pounce. That's when I slam him down my throat, hold him there, and swallow around his cock.

"*Fuck*, kitten." His hands hold me in position a moment longer before allowing me to pull back, but I don't give either of us much time before I eagerly deep throat him again. "That's right, kitten. Take the whole thing." He moans.

I carefully monitor my breathing as I move along his cock. I don't try to cover up or hide the sounds my body makes as he hits the back of my throat again and again.

Suddenly, he pulls me off of him. In the blink of an eye, I'm naked with my back pressed against the tree Malcolm was just lounging against. His lips are at my neck, and his cock is slamming into me.

"As much as I'd love to come in that pretty mouth, kitten," he grits out, "I'd much rather fill your tight pussy."

I bite my lip to keep my moans quiet as my fingers dig into his shoulders. He sets a brutal pace and makes sure to grind against my clit with each thrust.

"I want them to hear you, kitten." His demand wraps around me, feeling like an extra flick to my clit. "I want them to know you're getting fucked against a tree mere feet away from them."

I can't bite my lip in time to stop the moan that escapes me. He chuckles darkly as he continues to thrust into me.

"Louder, kitten."

He shifts so that my legs are hooked over his arms, allowing him to slide deeper into my pussy. My head falls back against the tree as I cry out. This position has him hitting every good spot inside me, even ones I didn't know I had.

"That's it, kitten." I can feel the bark digging into my back, but I don't care. All I care about is the sensation of his cock sliding along every nerve ending in my pussy. I clench tightly around him, causing him to let out a loud curse. "Good girl. Milk my cock."

I can't. It's too much. I barely register someone who sounds suspiciously like Ayla, yelling, "Finish her!" in her best Mortal Kombat voice.

I shatter. My scream rings out in the darkness around us, followed shortly after by Malcolm's roar as he finds his own release. My chest heaves against his as we both slowly come down from our pleasure filled high.

We just had sex outside with my family *literally feet away.* I'm both horrified and aroused.

His hand collars my throat, causing my eyes to focus on him. "No regrets, kitten."

Cheeky bastard had been listening to the bond. "No. Never any regrets. Though I'm sure I'll want to throttle you when my mother won't stop talking about this."

He chuckles as we both pull on our clothes. He grabs the nape of my neck and hauls me in for a crushing kiss that has me instantly melting against him all over again.

"At least I made sure no one was watching." My cheeks heat at his words. "Although, given your response, I think you might like it if someone watches." He shoots me a wink as he saunters back into the circle of light cast by the fire.

～

I HAD BEEN lucky enough not to run into my mother before Malcolm and I called it a night, though I'd run into Ayla who proclaimed Malcolm got a nine for overall performance. She subtracted one point because he hadn't bent me over in front of the entire village.

I'm now curled up against Malcolm, the early morning light filtering through the window of the hut we share.

"I cannot believe Ayla went all Mortal Kombat on us last night," I whisper aloud as memories of the previous evening's encounter against the tree play through my mind.

Malcolm's arm tightens around me as he laughs. "It added a nice touch to the finale."

I roll my eyes as I laugh. "Of course it did."

We get out of bed and prepare for the day, although neither one of us can avoid reaching out to touch or caress the other. Even though the threats we face still loom over our heads, it's easier to just *be* here.

We meet Ayla and Caleb outside our door. The pair seem to be wrapped up in their own little bubble, at least until Caleb spots Malcolm.

"Ballsy move, witch."

"You're just wishing you fucked Ayla up against a tree last night."

Oh. My. Gods. They were not smack talking about this in front of us.

"The entire New England pack heard my mate when I had her in the hallway."

"True. I'll have to make sure they hear Liv when we get back."

What. The. Fuck?

"I suggest," Ayla cuts in, "that neither one of you opens your mouth in front of us again if you both want to keep your dicks. Because right now, neither one of you is going to get laid for a very, *very* long time."

"She's right," I agree. My eyes narrow on Malcolm. "If you want to compare notes, do it without us around. Unless..." I pause, smirking over at Ayla. "You'd like *us* to do the same."

Ayla goes to say something, but Caleb slaps his hand over her mouth. Knowing her, whatever she'd been about to say would be far worse than what Caleb and Malcolm talked about.

"Fine," Caleb bites out. Malcolm nods, his eyes boring a hole through me. "Let's go meet up with your mother for a bit. She said something about a waterfall nearby."

I'm excited to explore the area again and have some time to just relax. We all need it. Aside from stolen moments here and there, we haven't actually stopped to rest since the battle in the Rockies. I can't believe it's only been a few months, it feels like that happened years ago.

"How soon do we think she's going to make a comment about you bumping nasties with Malcolm for the whole world to hear?" Ayla muses.

"The minute we walk through the door." I'm not even kidding.

"I think she's going to wait. Make you sweat it out," she replies. "She's going to wait until right before we walk out the door."

Ultimately, *Mama* and *Abuela* don't give us any additional information on the prophecy. They simply give us directions to the waterfall and tell us to relax. Not once does my mother mention what happened last night.

I'm instantly suspicious.

～

DESPITE SUSPECTING my mother and *abuela* are up to something, I float in the pool at the base of the waterfall. I know whatever they're up to, it's better left until later.

Hands wrap around my ankles and pull me under the surface of the water. Surprise flares through me, and I open my mouth to scream, but it fills with water. Thankfully I don't inhale. The hand releases me, and I shoot to the surface, coughing my brains out one I breach it.

I wipe the water from my eyes, and my gaze lands on a laughing Malcolm. He's a dead man. I gently tap on my bond with Ayla, quickly explaining what I want to do. Her agreement is instant.

Sweet, sweet revenge.

"*Pendejo*," I warn, "it's not nice to try to drown your mate."

"I did no such thing." He rolls his eyes, clearly thinking I'm being far too dramatic for what just happened.

"Whatever you want to call it" —a wide grin spreads across my face at the sight behind him— "retribution is swift."

Before he has a chance to respond, a large dragon claw pushes him underwater before wrapping around him and hoisting him into the air. He sputters in protest, but Caleb just drops him back into the water. I wince when Malcolm lands in a belly flop.

Pendejo deserved it.

Malcolm surges to the surface, his eyes narrowed into deadly slits. That's all it takes for me to lose it. Caleb shifts back and pulls his pants on, his booming laughter echoing around us.

"Just so we're all clear here," Malcolm growls, "you're all dead."

Ayla, kicking water in Malcolm's direction as she sits on the edge of the pool, laughs. "You're *so* scary." The sarcasm is thick enough to be sliced with a knife. "Whatever will I do with myself? I am so afraid."

My lips twitch as I try to stop more laughter from bubbling up. My mate looks ready to zap Ayla, but it's clear he knows better than to do it in front of Caleb. Maybe he's not smart enough and he'll do it in front of me. I'd have no problem getting revenge for her.

"Don't hate the player, witch, hate the game," I call out as I make my way out of the water.

I feel a small pang of guilt. I hope the others in New England have been able to take some time to relax. Now that we have the journal, we can head back home. I'm more eager for that than I am to stay and relax.

"What do you say we head home?" I beam at the agreements that chime back at me.

$$\sim$$

WHEN WE TELL my mother and *abuela* that we're heading back home they give me tight hugs. They both now what we're facing. I know that they believe in me, but they're realists too. We're up against steep odds. Assuming we make it out of this whole mess, I'm going to be spending more time with them.

"I promise to call more often." I squeeze *abuela*.

"Good, *mija*. At least that way we'll know that you aren't having loud sex with your mate." I can feel the heat creeping up my cheeks at my mother's proclamation. "The entire village heard you, *mija*!"

She comes over and lightly whacks me on the head. I grin back at her sheepishly. Malcolm lets out a loud belly laugh, only to be silenced when Mama shoots him a glare. She marches over to the witch and stabs his chest with her finger.

"You had better take care of my *mija*, do you understand?" He nods. "Good. If anything happens to her, I'm going to make sure that you don't have a dick to put in her."

I just want the ground to swallow me whole.

Chapter Thirteen

We're back on New England pack soil, and it feels great to be home. After visiting my family, we grabbed Fayden from Ireland and came back here. It feels important that we're all together for the next steps of this journey.

Especially after the bomb we dropped on Kelly a few days ago.

I glance up at the knock on my office door. Reading security reports from when we were gone isn't most people's idea of fun, but I love it. Xin is standing in the doorway with a young witch I've seen around town but haven't really had the chance to get to know. She isn't quite as tall as Kelly, but she has a similar willowy build. Her shoulder-length hair is done in a half up, half down style, and her bright green eyes shine with intelligence. I have a feeling I'm going to like her.

"Olivia," Xin begins, his smooth tenor floating over to me, "I have a small request, if you have time."

"Of course!" I gesture for them to take a seat in the two chairs stationed in front of my desk. "What can I help you with?"

"Ripley and I have been discussing better feeding arrangements for the vampires. We want to ensure all of our fighters are as well fed as possible considering the potential for multiple battles in the future." Xin and the witch, Ripley, take a seat.

I nod. It makes sense. While most vampires feed from human blood banks, it will make them more powerful if they feed off those in the community. We'd never really had a need for a blood bank before, but with a nest of vampires living with us now, it would be beneficial.

"I'm one of the healers," Ripley informs me. "I can easily organize a blood bank in the infirmary."

"Perfect. I'll clear my schedule so we can work out the details. Why don't the three of us tackle this together?"

"Thank you, Beta." Xin bows his head. Ripley has a small, pleased smile on her face.

Security isn't the only aspect of my job as beta. It's also important that I see to things like this too. I'm glad individuals in the community feel comfortable forming a plan and bringing it to me, especially newer members like Xin.

"I can't take anything off my plate today," I amend, "but starting tomorrow, I'm all yours. I'll let Ayla know what the plan is so we can make an announcement for donations tomorrow morning. Are the vampires all set for blood in the meantime?" I'm ashamed I even have to ask. I should know this.

Xin nods. "Yes. We brought quite a bit of human blood with us. We'll be fine until we have a solid supply of supernatural blood."

I quickly relay this information to Ayla through our bond, letting her know that we'll need to discuss logistics on blood donation tonight at dinner.

"And we have adequate storage for all new blood?" I'm not a healer by any means, and I'm not completely sure of our capacity to hold the amount of blood I'm sure we'll need to harvest, but I know this is a detail we can't overlook.

"I can create what we need without too much effort," Ripley responds. "We have the space for a facility next to the infirmary. I can get another witch or two to help me speed up the building process. We can have it ready by tomorrow afternoon."

"You work fast." That's good. She may look young, but she's clearly got her shit together.

"Stopping whatever is coming is extremely important," she states simply.

She's right. Stopping the Härja is the most important thing we may ever do. With that, they stand and leave. My thoughts start to race once they are gone. Is there anything else we're missing? Any other detail we've missed?

We're going to have more to talk about at dinner than just the blood bank. We can't let details like this go unattended. While a supernatural blood bank for our vampires may seem like a small detail since they are pretty damn strong without it, it could very well mean the difference between victory or death.

Goddess knows we need all the power we can possibly pack if we're going to have even the smallest shot at kicking ass. I tug on the end of my braid as I start to make a list of topics to cover.

LATER THAT DAY, after I've finished my paperwork and met with all of my team, I run through everything else I should get done before I tackle the blood bank tomorrow with Xin and Ripley. Thankfully there isn't much. The vampires are transitioning seamlessly into our society, we've got plenty of space for the Council, and our patrols haven't spotted any demon activity in the area.

I'm not sure if I should be relieved or worried about that last bit. We were attacked in Ireland, but not here. Will there be an attack now that we're back? I tug on my braid as I think about all the possibilities.

Malcolm said the group in Ireland had been a scouting party. It's possible they won't send another here.

How the hell did they know we were in Ireland?

I feel Malcolm brush against the bond. I must have leaked some of what I'm feeling. I brush back to let him know I'm fine. There's just too much to think about. I need to make a damn list or something.

I also think we need to switch tracks a bit. While finding Ayla's sisters is important, I think we need more information on just what the hell is going on first. That prophecy seems to suggest that Ayla and her sisters need to fall in some capacity. Her sisters can't do that if they are asleep, and we have no idea how to wake them up yet.

Malick and his allies don't want to kill Ayla or her sisters. They need them to open the gates to Hell, so it stands to reason that given my mother's vision, they are safe wherever they are for the time being.

I'm jittery with anxious energy, desperately wanting to physically do something. Strategy is part of my job for the pack, but I feel much better when I'm able to actually do something instead of just talking about it.

I make my way out of my office and into the kitchen of the packhouse. A snack and some coffee will help. As I rummage through the cabinets and pantry for what I want, I smell my mate as he walks into the room.

"I was just getting a snack and coffee. Want some?" I don't bother turning to look at him as I continue my search.

I feel the heat of his body as he appears behind me. His

arms wrap around me, pulling me flush against him. Grinding his into mine, Malcolm leans down to nibble on my ear. I shiver.

"I had a different sort of snack in mind." His husky voice goes right to my clit, and I arch back against him. He's rock hard against my ass, and I have to bite back a moan.

"What do you say, kitten?" He trails kisses down my neck. My head falls to the side to give him more room.

"What exactly did you have in mind?" My question is breathy with desire.

He cups me through my pants, his deft fingers rubbing my clit. I grip the shelf in front of me as I thrust back against him while also trying to arch into his hand. My body can't seem to make up its mind about where it wants to go.

All I know is that I just need to touch him.

"You should know by now, kitten, you're my favorite snack." Malcolm flicks my earlobe with his tongue before gently tugging on it with his teeth. "And I'm starving."

All of my hormones have taken up cheerleading. There isn't a part of me that has a problem with letting him make a feast of me, and after what happened back in my mother's village, I have no issue with him eating me out in the pantry here in the packhouse. At least it has a door.

"Yes," I moan.

Malcolm spins me around, dropping to his knees before me. His gaze travels the length of my body before locking on mine. His brown eyes, alight with heat, clash with my own, and a wicked smirk breaks out on Malcolm's face as he slowly unbuttons and unzips my pants.

I'm panting, but each breath doesn't provide nearly enough oxygen to my body as I watch him drag my jeans down my legs. He makes quick work of my shoes, and I lift each leg to allow him to remove my pants entirely. My panties are still on, and his gaze zeros in on the navy blue silk.

"I'm not sure if I want to leave these on or not," he rumbles against my thigh. His finger traces the seam, causing my hips to jerk in response.

In a blink, they are ripped from my body. My panther lets out a hungry rumble as Malcolm's face closes in on my pussy. She has no issue being this witch's snack. In fact, if it was up to her, he'd make a meal out of us at least three times a day.

Malcolm lifts my legs so they rest on his shoulders, and I bury my hands in his hair. He inhales deeply and groans. "I love the taste of you, kitten. Now be a good girl and come on my tongue."

I mean...okay.

He leans in and lashes my clit with his tongue. My breath leaves me in a rush, and my hips arch into his face. His chuckle vibrates against my clit as he continues to lick me like I'm the best damn snack he's ever had. Two fingers slowly slide into my pussy, and my head falls back against the shelves.

It's clear by the leisurely stroke of both his tongue and fingers that he wants to take his time and savor me, which seems at odds with his early demand that I come on his tongue, but I'm not about to complain. Especially not when his fingers curl against my G-spot at the same moment he starts to suck on my clit.

My legs start to shake as pleasure floods my body. All I can think about is the feel of him against me. His free hand slaps against my ass cheek. Once. Twice. Three times. I moan with each strike. I'm so close to hurtling over the edge.

Come for me, kitten, Malcolm demands. His teeth scrape against my clit at the same time he rubs my G-spot and slaps my ass again.

My grip on his hair tautens, and I'm sure it's painful as my pussy clenches tightly around his fingers. The orgasm that washes through me is so intense, I feel like I'm going to combust. I don't know if I make a sound as I come, too lost in the sensations coursing through my body.

Malcolm laps up every drop, never once stopping his fingers or his tongue as we ride out my orgasm. He lets my legs slide from his shoulders then lifts me as he slams his lips onto mine.

Again, kitten. This time he lays me on a flat surface. We're still in the kitchen, but he's moved us to the large island that rests in the middle of the space.

With a snap of his fingers, our clothes are gone. He once again drops to his knees, and his mouth returns to the task of making me scream.

Two fingers make their way back into my dripping pussy. He doesn't brush against my G-spot this time. Torture it is then. I prop myself on my elbows so I can watch as he eats me out. His chocolate brown eyes glitter in the light of the kitchen, and the heat I see in them has my pussy fluttering and my back arching enticingly.

I want him to get down to business. Unfortunately, he seems content to take his time. And we're in the middle of the damn kitchen where anyone can see us—I'm both mortified and extremely turned on by the thought.

Malcom's magic starts to play with my nipples with the same leisurely pace that's been driving me insane. The buildup is slow but powerful. I just want him to let me fall, damn it!

Just when I'm about to topple over the edge, *finally*, Malcolm stops. I'm too shocked to threaten him properly, only emitting a low growl. He ignores the threat and kisses his way up my body, wrapping my legs around his hips as he goes.

I whimper at the feel of his cock brushing against my clit and try to angle my hips so he'll slip inside me. Thwarting my efforts, Malcolm pulls his hips back ever so slightly.

"Did you want something, kitten?"

I'm going to murder him. "I want your cock, you asshole."

He tsks. "That's no way to ask nicely."

I growl again.

A squeak leaves my lips when Malcolm pulls away from me and takes me off the island, spinning me so my torso is bent over the cool marble there. The sharp sting of his hand on my ass has me gasping and my hips jerking back against him.

"I told you that wasn't any way to ask for my cock, kitten," he says in a low growl. Another slap, this time on the other cheek, has me biting back a moan. "Now, do you want my cock?"

I whimper and nod, unable to form the necessary words to answer him properly. Two more slaps on each cheek have me releasing a low moan.

"Ask *nicely*, kitten."

"Please." My voice is breathy and low. "I need your cock."

"Where do you need it?"

I balk at the question. He's always been the one to talk to me during sex. I've never been a dirty talker...or much of a talker at all during sex.

Two more slaps.

"Where do you need my cock, kitten."

"My pussy," I whisper.

He kneads the globes of my ass as he spreads my legs a little wider, allowing him to slide his cock against my pussy more easily. My hips have a mind of their own and move back toward him, begging for him to fill me.

"I'll let you get away with that today, but you're going to have to ask me louder next time, kitten." His tone is dark and dangerous, filled with so much heat that my desire skyrockets.

"Please," I murmur. I *need* him to fill me just as badly as I need my next breath.

"I've got you, kitten." With that, he slowly, painstakingly, slides into my aching core.

I want to sob at the feeling of him filling me, stretching me in the most delicious way possible. He hits every nerve ending. A soft *thud* fills the silence when my head falls to the counter. Malcom's hands tangle in my hair, pulling my head up, while his other hand circles my waist so his fingers can play with my clit.

"You don't get to come until I say so, kitten," he whispers against my ear. His chest is now flush with my back, and he's moving out of me with that same, slow, agonizing pace.

I try to nod, but his grip on my hair prevents me from moving too much. He gets my message though. "Good girl."

He slams into me, causing me to cry out in surprise. His fingers start to work my clit as he sets a brutal pace. My hips hit the island with each thrust, my nipples skimming the cool counter.

I feel my orgasm building rapidly, and my pussy starts to flutter wildly around Malcolm's cock. He grunts, picking up his pace.

"Not until I say so," he grits out.

I whimper, desperately trying to hold off my orgasm for as long as possible. I think it may kill me. The pleasure is blinding, and it rings through every cell in my body.

"Malcolm!" My tone is a plea for salvation.

"Not yet."

He continues to pound into me. I'm nearly mindless, calling out his name like a prayer. I can't hold my orgasm back. I start to come with such amazing force—

Malcolm stops moving. His teeth dig into my shoulder, and he removes his hand from my clit to slap my ass several times.

"What did I say, kitten?"

I try to focus on what he asked, but I'm still so close to coming that I have a hard time processing his words.

"I said you couldn't come until I told you to." He punctuates that statement with a sharp thrust of his hips. I cry out because it only serves to bring me that much closer. "Did I say you could come yet?"

I'm trying to move my hips against his, trying to get any sort of friction to reach that last step. I need to come so badly.

"Did I?" he snarls.

I shake my head, allowing my body to go limp.

He starts to slowly, gently thrust against me again. It keeps the buildup going, but it isn't nearly enough to push me over the edge.

Malcolm pulls my hair, guiding me up so my back is flush against his chest as he settles upright. His hot breath wafts against my ear, and it causes me to shiver. He's returning to that brutal pace, the one I need to come.

His fingers find their way back to my clit. "Okay, kitten. You can come."

With only a few more thrusts, I'm screaming his name to the heavens as my pussy grips his cock in a stranglehold. I literally see fireworks. *Dios Mío. Am I dead?*

Malcolm groans as he comes moments later, telling me I'm still alive. We collapse against the top of the island, his weight comforting instead of crushing.

"Why the fuck do I always walk in on people fucking?" The male voice startles me, and my head whips around to see Connor leaning against the wall near the door. He's got a broad grin on his face. "First, Caleb and Ayla in the hallway, and now you two." He shakes his head. "It's not fair, if you ask me. And we all make food on that!"

Malcolm doesn't seem surprised by his friend's presence.

He knew Connor was there. I sort of want to die. How long has he been there? I'm not sure I want to know.

"I walked in on Caleb and Ayla once too," Malcolm states with a chuckle. "And your time will come, brother."

Connor chuckles and walks out the door.

Chapter Fourteen

I'm still not sure if I want to find a hole to die in. I knew having sex with Malcolm in the kitchen could mean someone would see us. I hadn't cared—at least, not until someone *had* seen us.

And both of them have caught Caleb and Ayla? Did Ayla know about that? I doubt it, or she would have told me.

Looks like I have one more thing to add to my list of topics to discuss with her. My lips twitch. She's going to kill all three of them.

"What else do you need to do today?" Malcolm's voice is low as he peppers a few kisses along my shoulder. We're not in the kitchen anymore. He followed me back to my office once we'd tracked down our clothes.

"Just a few more odds and ends. I really need to talk to Ayla. We've got a few community issues we need to discuss. You, Connor, and Caleb should be there too. We'll have a few Council related questions." I try not to lean back against him. We don't have time for another round. At least, not until tonight.

"I can make sure they're there." He nips my neck, sending shivers down my spine.

"Malcolm," I chide, a smile twitching on my lips. "I do need to actually finish a few things today."

"Mmm." He nuzzles against me before sighing loudly and pulling away. "I suppose if you're going to be responsible, I should be too."

I laugh at that. "It's not like we're in a life-or-death struggle against some boss bad guy or anything." I roll my eyes at him.

"Nah." He grins at me as he heads out the door.

I've never felt happiness like this before, never felt like I truly belonged with someone. Malcolm is everything I never knew I needed and more. Life certainly isn't going to be dull with him. I wonder if this is how Caleb feels about Ayla. The thought makes me chuckle.

Beta to Supreme Ruler. Come in, Supreme Ruler. Over, I project to Ayla with a laugh.

Supreme Ruler to Beta, I read you. Over. She's playing along like I knew she would. Bless.

I request a meeting.

Request granted. I'll be there in a minute.

All hail the Supreme Ruler. Over.

Ayla pokes her head into my office a minute later, her eyes dancing with laughter. She plops herself in one of the chairs opposite me. "What can I do for you as your supreme ruler?"

She's going to milk this until it's so dead it's dust.

"I've got a few things I want to cover with you before we discuss them with the rest of the gang." I pull out my notebook, and Ayla groans.

"She even brings out the notebook. This is going to be *great*." I can feel her excitement through the bond despite her words. We've been so focused on this whole demon and Hell thing that we haven't been able to focus on settling the community we're trying to build.

"Xin and a young witch named Ripley suggested a supernatural blood bank for the vamps. It'll give them an extra boost for battle. They are working out some of the logistics, but we're going to need to make the announcement and ask for volunteers.

"We also need to discuss general community protections now that our numbers have grown. We should get more people on the security team and start working out a better rotation. We should take more of the Council settling here into consideration now that it's going to be disbanding.

"On that note, do we know when we want to dissolve the Council? And how many more are coming to settle here? We may need to expand the town, upgrade some of our facilities, and expand the infirmary, things like that.

"We need to do a supply inventory and have members who regularly go into the city bring necessary items back. But we shouldn't do that until after we determine how many new residents we're going to have or anticipate having."

Ayla nods, holding a notebook and pen in her hands as she scribbles notes of her own. "Anything else?"

"A few non-community specifics." I sigh and lean back in my seat. "We need to figure out how the demons knew we were in Ireland, touch base with Fayden about how her set up is going and the journal entries, and we need to have a girl chat with Kelly about being a sin eater. I haven't seen her since we got back."

Ayla winces. "Neither have I. I feel horrible about it, but I think she's avoiding us."

"It's a lot to process. We've all realized that our parents have lied to us about this whole shitshow. Not to mention we're gaining new powers, and it's the first time many of us have actually fought. I don't blame her for wanting time to herself."

"Neither do I," Ayla murmurs, "but that doesn't mean I'm not worried about her."

"Well, let's go check on her now," I suggest. I stand, and Ayla does the same. "I feel her at home."

"Let's do this."

WE'RE STANDING in front of Kelly's door. She doesn't live in the packhouse. Her house is about a block away and tucked back enough that she's got plenty of privacy. I can't hear anyone moving around inside, which has me mildly concerned.

Ayla and I exchange a glance before she knocks. Nothing.

"Kelly, open the damn door!" Ayla knocks again. "We know you're in there. Don't make me break this damn door down."

"She'll do it!" I yell. "You know she will!"

A string of curses rings out, followed by hurried foot-steps. Kelly rips the door open, wearing a scowl on her face.

Dios Mío, she looks rough. Oh, my poor sister.

Her hair is disheveled, her eyes look like someone punched her, her skin is pale and lacking her normal glow, and she's lost weight. *Fuck.*

We're shitty friends. I feel horrible that I've let her get this bad. *We should have been here before now.*

She's blocked the bond, and there was a lot to deal with. Don't be too hard on yourself, my panther soothes, but I can feel Ayla's guilt too, which adds to my own.

"Hey, love." Ayla moves to wrap her arms around Kelly. I step behind her and hug both of them. "We're here now."

A deep shuddering breath leaves Kelly. Her arms encircle us and her body starts to shake.

"Shh," I murmur. "You're not going through this alone. We promise."

Suddenly, I feel Darcy behind me, joining in on our group hug. "No," she agrees, "we're all here for you."

Things already feel better.

We slowly untangle ourselves and move into Kelly's living room. I tuck her into her papasan chair and go to get her some tea. I'm learning that we can't keep trying to spare each other from our shit. We're best friends, sisters, and we need to be able to rely on one another to get us through this.

My mate bond with Malcolm is vastly different than what I have with these women. My sisters are the foundation of my strength. Malcolm helps to strengthen me, but these three, right here, are my base, my rock, and I can't forget that.

I hand Kelly her tea and take a seat on the couch with Ayla and Darcy. It's silent for a moment, all of us lost in our own thoughts.

"I should have said I needed help sooner," Kelly whispers, her eyes locked on her tea. "I hadn't realized how hard this was hitting me until I heard you knocking on my door."

Shame floods our bond.

"There's nothing to be ashamed of," I state. "This entire thing has been so hard for all of us, and we've all gotten lost in our own heads. It isn't just you, but it's so important to know you aren't going through this alone."

Kelly looks up and locks gazes with each of us, a small smile tugging at her lips.

"Now, tell us what happened with your mother." I get up and move to sit on the floor by her legs, wrapping my arm around her calf and leaning my head against her knee. Shifters touch to soothe. While Kelly is a witch, touch is still a very human element that comforts someone.

Kelly takes a long pull of her tea before she starts. "My mother said her line descends from one of the original sin eater lines. When they were being hunted, she said they started suppressing that trait. My grandmother was the first descendent born without the power, and they all thought it had finally been stripped from us by the gods. My mother doesn't have the power either.

"They thought it skipped me too... until I was one. I accidentally pulled a sin from a human." Oh gods. That could easily kill a human. "My mother felt the boost in my power, saw what happened to the human, and put two and two together."

"Shit," Darcy mutters. "I'm surprised the human was still alive. You were so young with no control."

"That's what my mom said. I guess I only pulled a small amount of envy from him. She panicked. She rushed me home to Dad and they bound that part of me. They decided they wouldn't mention it at all until I confronted them the other day." She sighs and tries to run her hand through her hair. Encountering several knots, she scowls. "I should probably shower."

I move away from her legs to let her stand.

"I know I have more to talk about, but...I feel gross."

"Go shower," Ayla says. "We'll be here."

KELLY SPENDS ABOUT HALF an hour in the shower. I can't blame her. I'd be in there scrubbing myself until I was red.

She comes padding out of the bathroom, her hair wrapped in a towel, dressed in leggings and a baggy shirt. Thank the gods she looks much better than she did when she answered the door. She still has black bags under her eyes, but they have a little more life in them than they did before, and her skin is flush from the heat of the shower.

My shoulders relax as she comes back to the papasan. I hadn't realized how tense I'd been, but seeing her marginally more like herself is a huge relief.

"My parents hadn't realized that my being a sin eater was connected to what's going on," she starts. "I told her about how I'd eventually come into my queen powers, but it didn't dawn on her to mention my other abilities. I guess because they'd been bound for so long without incident, she honestly didn't think to mention them." She seems as though she doesn't quite believe her mother. She sounds angry and betrayed.

Emotions Ayla and I have felt recently too. It kills me that our friend has to feel like this as well.

"They can't remove the binding." Kelly takes her hair out of the towel and starts to run her fingers through her honey gold locks. "They aren't strong enough now. I guess I'll have to see if the binding will break when I come into my new powers."

"We can try to break the binding if you want," Ayla offers.

Kelly shakes her head. "Not yet. I want to wait. I'm...I'm not sure what will happen." Her eyes find mine. "I hope I come into my powers on the battlefield against the demons the same way Olivia did. That way if I hurt anyone, it'll most likely be an enemy instead of a friend."

"Fair enough." I can see the logic in that. "We'll wait."

"Would you like me to tell you what I know of the sin eaters?" Darcy inquires. Our gazes turn to her in curiosity. I keep forgetting she's an original. The first witch *and* the first vampire. She's seen it all.

"Please." Kelly smiles at her. It's the first real smile we've seen from her. I relax a bit more at the sight. Out of the corner of my eye, I see Ayla relax visibly as well.

Darcy sits forward, her elbows on her knees. "Sin eaters were a special breed of witches, not born of my bloodline. They came from Jesus' bloodline."

Wait a minute. I hold up my hands. "*The* Jesus?"

Darcy's lips twitch. "Yes, *the* Jesus. He was a guardian. One of the first witches."

"I'm sorry..." My brain must be offline. "Did you just say Jesus was a *witch*?"

Darcy's laugh echoes through the living room. "He was a guardian, just as I was. We all have our roles to play. He was devoted to the god who created him. His sacrifice was important." She pauses, a frown marring her features. She shakes her head. "Anyway, he was the first sin eater. They were meant to aid in the fight against demons. Demons were born from mortal souls that had been led astray and could not be reborn because of this. A sin eater can rip the sin from that soul and effectively...reset, for lack of a better word, that soul. They will start their reincarnation chain all over again.

"If the sin eater pulls too much, they can destroy the soul altogether. That was part of why they were hunted not just by demons, but supernaturals as well. Sin eaters learned that they could eat the sins of mortals and supernaturals. Those who had been tainted by demons carry the same stain."

"I've seen that taint," Ayla interjects. "They appear... fuzzy? Almost like I can't quite focus on them, or like they are ink on a page that has been smudged. That's how I knew which trail to follow when I first got involved with Kelly and Olivia. Well, I figured it out along the way anyway."

Darcy nods. "It makes sense that a queen would be able to see the stain or sense it. It's possible for a supernatural to work for a demon without tainting themselves. So long as they aren't doing the killing or dark magic themselves, they won't show the taint that those who have dabbled do."

"So you're telling me that I can rip the sins out of demons? Kill them? Just like that?" Kelly sounds astonished.

"It's not quite that simple," Darcy cautions, "but without you being able to feel your powers, yes. That's the basics of sin eating. I'm not entirely sure *how* you do that. All I know is that you'll be able to sense or feel the sin and then take it into yourself. You're then able to convert that energy into something you can use. The soul should then be released back into the universe to begin anew."

"*Mierda*," I whisper. Kelly is badass.

"You'll need to be careful not to take too much," Darcy warns. "Too much power can kill you."

That sobers us all.

I'm not sure any of us are certain what our limits are, but the thought of an overload is scary. Do we just...explode? What happens? I shake myself out of those thoughts. I don't think I want to know.

Chapter Fifteen

We spend some time reconnecting at Kelly's house. It's easy to forget how much your friends lift your spirits and soothe your soul when you're buried under piles of crap. But the second you reconnect with them, everything seems right in the world again.

We're heading to the packhouse to meet with Malcolm and the others for dinner. We'll need to talk to them about what the Council's plans are, but compared to what we just dealt with, I'm not as concerned about their answers.

"I've been thinking," Darcy says as we take our time walking home. "Ayla said queens historically took alpha dragons as their mates."

"But we were also historically only female dragons," Ayla points out. "You three aren't dragon shifters."

"You're right," Darcy agrees. "I think the gods are diversifying. Olivia is a panther shifter, Kelly is a witch, and I'm a vampire."

"You're a weird hybrid of basically everything," I tease. "But you're right."

"When I was being held by Malick, right after the goddesses saved me..." Ayla pauses to take a deep breath. "They showed me my mother's fate. Katja said that queens, dragons, shouldn't be the only ones to have power like that. Honestly, I completely agree. I don't agree with how she went about trying to get that kind of power, but I've never thought dragons should be the only ones to be at the top of the food chain, so to speak."

"I know there's a prophecy and all that," Kelly says, "but what if the gods are...I don't know...changing fate as they go? Olivia doesn't have an alpha dragon as a mate. Darcy and I might not either. We all know how hard it is for normal supernaturals to find their mates."

I've been thinking about this deep in the recesses of my mind. There are so many things that can block a mate bond, such as insecurities or being from a different species. In those cases, the bond takes a while to form. The couple often doesn't feel an instant connection, which is what happened with Malcolm and me. I felt a pull toward him before I'd come into my queen powers, but the knowledge that he was my mate didn't fully hit me until that day on the battlefield.

"I've talked to my dragon a bit about this," Ayla comments. "She says it's part of the queen magic. The bond forms automatically without either party really putting any effort in. Obviously, the pair has to work to make it finalize, but there aren't the same hindrances that other supernaturals have. Something to do with boosting a queen's power. We're more powerful when we're bonded with our mate." She shrugs. "At least that's what she tells me."

"Interesting," Darcy murmurs. "So it's possible Kelly and I won't know who our mates are—if we know them already, that is—until our powers come in."

Ayla nods. "Yeah. Unless you overcome those hurdles

beforehand, I think you're right. You're still just normal supernaturals right now."

"I wonder what will happen once this is all over." I look at the others as they all turn their attention to me. "Will the gods continue to allow new queens from different species and allow them to take mates who aren't alpha dragons? Or will they go back to only having dragon shifters as queens? If so, will our powers be stripped?"

"I don't think I want to worry about that right now," Kelly mutters. "We have way too much on our plate to contemplate something that far in the future."

She's right. It's part of my job to think about things like this though, so it's hard to turn off that part of my brain. It's a mix of being head of security and being a tight little ball of anxiety. At least I'm self-aware.

We make our way into the dining room to find the guys, as well as Xin, Ripley, and Fayden, all seated at the table. I'm surprised to see Ripley but pleased because I'll be able to get an update on how things went today, and Ayla and I can call a meeting for tomorrow first thing in the morning.

When my gaze lands on Connor, I fight the urge to blush, but he doesn't look at me or Malcolm. His gaze is fixed on Kelly. His gaze is almost predatory as he watches her take her seat. There's concern there too. My eyes flick over to my friend. She isn't paying any attention to the dire wolf, almost as though she's purposely avoiding his gaze.

You seeing this? I address Ayla and Darcy. I notice both of them covertly glance between the shifter and witch, their interest instantly piqued.

Something is going on between those two. If I'm right, it's the same something that happened between Malcolm and me before I came into my powers and realized we were mates.

Well, hot damn! I'm excited for Kelly, but I can tell she's not ready yet. She'll need a bit more time before Connor can act on that animal instinct he's feeling. There's a part of me that's just screaming at them to kiss in my head, but I'll leave it be for now. I can hardcore ship them from a distance until it actually happens.

"We've got a lot to talk about, so let's dig in." Ayla gestures for everyone to eat.

As we're eating, we discuss the plans for the blood bank, which Ripley confirms is almost finished. Ayla, Kelly, Dante, and I agree to make an announcement in the morning to get volunteers to give blood. We're all sure there won't be an issue there.

I tell Caleb we need to go over plans for the dissolution of the Council so we can plan for more community members here in town. This opens up a whole new can of worms. Are we going to have branches of this community throughout the rest of the world? There will eventually be six queens, so are we all going to stay here? What will the new governing body really look like? Will it just be queens at the table, or will we have others as well?

I knew this process would take time, and I knew I was going to be part of the process since I'm now a queen, but dear goddess, I'd rather leave this to someone else.

We agree to come back to this topic at a later date once we've all had time to think about the options, plus we still have more to discuss.

"What I really want to know," I begin, "is how the hell those demons knew where we were when we were in Ireland. That cottage is still warded to high heaven."

"We've been trying to figure that out," Fayden chimes in. She's practically bouncing in her seat. "While my tech struggled with your memories, Olivia, it does suggest there may be a mole in either the community or the Council. The other probability is that Malick is able to watch us without a mole, that he's gained a new ability somehow, which isn't out of the realm of possibility."

A heavy silence greets her. A mole is my worst fear. Then again, so is Malick gaining new abilities. We still don't know for sure who saved him during that battle outside his facility. We speculated that it might be one of the Härja, but we haven't figured that out for sure yet. If his friend is able to give him new powers, we're even more fucked than we thought.

"I know we threw out the idea that Malick could be working with the Härja," I muse, "but we didn't really flesh that out much. It makes sense, right?" I look around the table. "I mean, based on what we know. Malick has claimed that he wants to open the gates of Hell to let Lucifer out, but Ayla and I saw Lucifer volunteer to create a prison for the Härja.

"It's possible one of the Härja has been acting as Lucifer to get Malick to open the gates," I continue as my brain starts to work through everything we've experienced. "Or Malick is lying about why he wants to open the gates. Either way, I think it's safe to assume Malick has ties to the Härja."

Ayla nods thoughtfully. "I agree. Brigid said Malick wasn't the main threat, but she wouldn't tell me exactly what was. Then we were pulled into that vision in Ireland. The Härja are the main threat. The prophecy suggests that by the three Fates falling, the gates to Hell will open and they'll be unleashed. But what exactly does it mean by Fates falling?"

"There are a few meanings," Fayden supplies. "One is that the Fates all die. Another is a fall from grace sort of situation —think how popular literature now has Lucifer falling from Heaven. A third is a loss of power."

"How are we supposed to stop the Fates from falling if we don't know what the hell that actually means?" Caleb's gruff response has us all pausing. I'm sure we were all thinking the same thing.

"Fayden," Malcolm says, breaking the silence, "you're taking notes on all this, right?" She nods. "Good. We need a new way of seeing all these facts. Can you play with that?"

"Sure." Her fingers start flying across her tablet.

"Let's bookmark this." Everyone agrees. "Great. Can I have my *abuela's* journal?"

Fayden slides it across the table. It's thicker than most, with pages that have been sewn in as my *abuela* continued to collect information she thought was important. Most of the pages are yellowed with age, and the soft brown leather is worn along the creases.

"What did you find out?" I ask.

Fayden taps at her tablet a bit before settling on something. "There's a lot packed into that journal, but I'll give you as much of the CliffsNotes version as I can. It's still going to be long though. Feel free to interrupt me with questions."

We all nod.

"I think the best place to start is with what your *abuela* had on the gods, then we can work on queens and their origins, demons, and then the prophecy. There's really no linear outline to the journal, but I tried to organize the topics as best as I could.

"From what your *abuela* could gather, the gods once called Earth home before they created their own realm. Christianity calls that realm Heaven, and that seems to be the most well-known name for it, so I'm going to stick with that. Their exact origins are unknown, and your *abuela* speculated that *they* don't even know their own origins anymore.

"At some point, there was a divide between them, and they waged war against each other for an eternity before the gods finally created their own realm. Your *abuela* doesn't say anything about this, so I'm just making assumptions here, but it's possible they fought for so long because they either hoped they would be able to kill each other off, or because neither group knew how to create a realm before that point. I'm not sure if that's important, but I've noted it just in case.

"Your *abuela* records here, several times, that the gods refuse to mess with free will. They'll blur the lines, so to speak, but they won't ever outright interfere, which is why I think this whole thing is just a complete mess. They don't want to mess with our free will, but they do want to help us protect the balance. They walk a weird line. Very blurry."

That's not news. We'd been wondering why this whole thing was just a bunch of crap to wade through, and if what my *abuela* had in this journal was right, "free will" was the reason. A shit reason, but a reason.

"Based on a rough timeline which I sort of had to piece together, it was *after* the gods created and fled to their own realm that they created supernaturals. From what was gathered, the gods created supernaturals as guardians for mortals. Mortals came sometime after the creation of supernaturals."

"That's correct," Darcy interjects. "My memories of that time have faded, but I do know we are the guardians of mortals. We're meant to protect them from demons."

"That's murky," Fayden responds. "It seems like that's what ultimately happened, but the journal neither confirms nor denies that theory. I'm just not sure, because based on the vision from Ireland, the guardians were tasked with fighting the Härja, who had split from the gods. They possibly imprisoned them, but I couldn't find out if it was the guardians or the gods who ultimately did that. The vision suggests the guardians did that, but considering we're not gods, I'm just not sure.

"Anyway, the journal suggests that the gods gave each guardian line a small bit of their power, which is how we became what we are. As lines died out, so too did those powers, but our purpose remained the same—protect the mortals from corruption. It's unclear exactly *when* queens came into the picture and whether or not the Fates predate the queens or vice versa, but the Fates have only ever been chosen from queens. Queens have always had the ability to sense demons and battle against archdemons.

"This is where things get *really* interesting." She wiggles excitedly in her seat. "Mortal souls travel along a reincarnation cycle. It's not clear how many lives they have to live, but they travel along this cycle that ends in three ways—becoming a demon, becoming a guardian, or becoming 'enlightened.' It's unclear what the hell becoming enlightened means, but that seems to be the end goal of the whole process. At least according to the gods."

We're all leaning forward in our seats. I don't think any of us have heard this before. Darcy may remember some of this, but possibly not all of it. I'm not surprised she doesn't really recollect the beginning. It's been a hell of a long time. That's *way* too much information to store in any brain, even a supernatural and magical one.

"Corruption of the mortal soul leads to demons. This ends the reincarnation cycle for them. The guardians are meant to help prevent this. I'm going to go into what happens once they become demons more in a minute, so stick a pin in this. Exceptionally brave mortal souls are reborn as guardians.

"While guardians are only ever reborn as guardians, it seems like we have a shelf life. Again, I'm not sure how many lives we get to live, but it's finite, so the gods wanted a way to replenish our numbers without having to continue to create us from scratch. Honestly, this whole process just seems arbitrary, but hey, I'm not a god so I can't create the rules. So to recap...Enlightenment is the big end goal for a mortal soul. We, as guardians, are meant to ensure that a soul continues on its reincarnation cycle until that happens. We're meant to help prevent corruption. If that happens, demons are created. We then step in to prevent more corruption, because that is bad for the balance."

Okay, so if I have this right, the gods won't directly interfere with free will, but they seem to have put fail-safes in place to ensure the balance between good and evil, or light and dark, is kept and not skewed. This feels like we're some sort of weird high school science experiment. I'm not sure I like it.

"Let's move on to demons." Fayden taps her tablet. "This is where things start to tie in a bit more."

Chapter Sixteen

We're all eager to hear what else Fayden has to say. The curiosity saturating the room is palpable. Was it Sun Tzu who said something along the lines of understanding one's enemies? The more you know the better you're able to kill them. Pretty sure that's a direct quote.

Fayden breaks me out of my musings. "As I said, corrupt mortal souls turn into demons when they die, ending the reincarnation cycle. As a demon gains power, they become stronger, and if they aren't taken out by a sin eater they eventually become an archdemon.

"Sin eaters came into being to help *reset* demons and bring them *back* into the reincarnation cycle, which explains why they were hunted. That's some insane power. They were meant to help maintain the balance. The more corruption there is, the more the balance is tipped in that direction. If a supernatural other than a sin eater kills a demon, the soul is destroyed, not reset."

I'm...not sure how I feel about that. Even though it's now

a demon soul, it was once a human soul and could be reset to be mortal again.

"They don't originate in hell and never step foot there," Fayden continues. "They can turn into a demon at any time. There's really no point in the cycle where they are ensured to become enlightened."

I'm pretty sure I hear crickets. Everyone is trying to process. How had so much of this information just disappeared? Why would the gods allow that?

I understand why Kelly is a sin eater, whereas her mother and grandmother aren't. We're going to need her to seriously kick demon ass. We also now have an explanation for why the gods are essentially useless.

"Let's hit the pause button for a bit," Ayla says. "I know we still need to go through information on the prophecy and my sisters' locations, but let's make all of this a little more digestible."

"We still haven't found any answer as to *who* the Härja are," I state. "We know they are the same species as the gods, but...aside from that rift, how did they change so much? What are they now?"

Kelly hums in agreement. "Are they still the same species, and if so, do the same things that kill the gods kill them? Do we even know if the gods can be killed? Are we simply supposed to stop the Härja from getting out of Hell, or do we actually need to kill them? We're assuming we need to kill them, but it's entirely possible that's not necessary."

"I have found a reference regarding weapons that can kill the gods," Connor chimes in. "We'd have to confirm that they'll be effective. That is, if the gods are willing to share that information."

"At this point they'd better be," I argue. "We're pawns for them in this little chess game. Everything we've learned has been through some third-party source, not directly from them. They can do us this one solid."

The table is silent. Shock registers on a few faces, but for the most part, everyone seems more contemplative.

"I'm mildly surprised you didn't just burst into flames," Dante teases with a laugh. "I'm sure we all feel the same way to varying degrees, but voicing it outright like that takes some serious balls."

"Not really." I shrug. "They're all about free will. That comes with the allowance for being frustrated with them."

"I think there are still some serious holes in our information," Fayden says, breaking the silence caused by my last comment. "I'm sure most of the real information has been lost to time. Even Darcy, an original, doesn't have all the answers because it's been so long."

"Most of my memories from that time are hazy at best," Darcy admits.

"How do we want to move forward?" Ayla inquires. "Do we want to do a bit more digging into the weapons Connor mentioned, or do we want to go right for my sisters?" She turns to face Kelly. "Have you been able to make any headway on how to wake them once we've found them?"

"I have a few ideas" —Kelly shrugs— "but until I see them, I won't know for sure what your mother did to them and what's required to wake them."

"I think it's best," Malcolm reasons, "to dig a little more into whatever weapons we can get our hands on that may help tip the tide in our favor. It's paramount we try to keep Hell from releasing the Härja, but we should also be prepared for any eventuality. The prophecy is pretty vague in regard to whether or not we're actually going to have a serious battle."

Caleb nods before responding, "I agree. I want us all to have as many backup plans as we can get and be as ready as possible. That means training every single day until we leave to find the weapons and Ayla's sisters. It means making sure that our defenses are the strongest we can make them, that we have all the supplies we'll need, everything."

Ayla has an amused smile on her face. "And here I thought *I* was the queen in charge of this operation." She cuts me a look. "With Olivia, of course."

I laugh and wave her off.

We spend several hours planning the next week or so out. It'll take Connor at least that long to do more research on the weapons and hopefully discover their whereabouts. In the meantime, the rest of us have what seems like an insurmountable task on our plates—getting ready for a war we're not sure we can ever be remotely prepared for.

LATER THAT NIGHT, Ayla, Kelly, Darcy, and I are in Ayla's sitting room. We need to just be girlfriends again for a small amount of time. Our sisterhood is what will get us through this, I have no doubt about that. We'll stand, and possibly fall, together. Always.

"I think one of us should try to reach out to Brigid," Ayla murmurs as she leans back against the couch, staring up at the ceiling. "She might not give us an answer about those weapons, but nothing ventured, nothing gained, right?"

We all mumble our agreement.

"And I think it should be Liv who tries," Kelly blurts. My head whips around so I can drill her with my most intimidating glare. The bitch just ignores it. "Given how outspoken you've been, I think it may be best."

"How do you figure?" My brow rises. Maybe learning she's a sin eater has scrambled her brain a bit.

"Being so out of tune with something that's so fundamental for us makes it difficult to connect with your true source of power. I know you've been training with your magic, and Ayla has been trying to teach you how to fly, but have you really been able to tap into your power base since your queen powers emerged?"

I take a moment to think about that. While I've never felt stronger, Kelly has a point. I've seen firsthand the kind of power Ayla wields, and I haven't tapped into anything even remotely the same caliber. Are my feelings about the gods causing a disconnect with my abilities? The thought makes me feel a bit bitter.

"I see your point," I finally admit. "I'll try."

They all smile at me. "I have some tea that will help. It's meant to put you in a clear frame of mind when you fall asleep. It'll be easier to reach out to the goddess that way."

This woman and her tea. I fight the urge to roll my eyes. "Thanks, Kel." To my surprise, she hands over a small packet of tea. "You just...carry this around with you?"

"Something told me I might need it." She shrugs. Okay, so she just casually carries around random tea packets. What else does she tote around? The thought of my friend being some magical drug dealer makes me snort.

"Well..." I stand and stretch. "I may as well get to it. I'll have Malcolm watch over me."

"Don't stay up too late playing hide the pickle!" Ayla yells.

"What the actual fuck is wrong with you?" I laugh and shake my head as I leave the room, their laughter following me out.

I stare at the little packet in my hand as I make my way to my room. I can do this. I can totally do this. I'll just casually slip into a coma and then talk to a goddess. What could go wrong?

I groan and pull on the end of my braid. *Just don't insult the goddess while talking to her*, I remind myself. That should be easy, right?

As I step into my room, my gaze lifts to find a very naked Malcolm sprawled on my bed. The little hussy in me sits up to cheer, but I beat her back. As much as I'd like to just maul that man like the cat shifter I am, I want to actually do this whole goddess talk thing right away.

I strip out of my clothes far more slowly than I should, given I'm not going to be entertaining the heat in Malcolm's eyes, but it's fun to just watch him watching me. His entire attention is riveted to every move I make. He looks at me like he wants to eat me whole, and I'm here for it.

"We're going to have to hold off." I sigh and hold up the tea. "I need to have a little chat with Brigid."

Malcolm glances from me to the packet, his brow raised in question. "Do you now?"

"Yup. Need to have a heart-to-heart and then ask her about those weapons Connor is researching." I flop onto the bed next to him. "Can you magic me a cup of hot water?"

"You do it." I knew he was going to say that. He's been pushing me to use more and more magic for even the smallest things so I can practice.

I allow the magic to swirl inside me as I think about what I want it to do. I picture a steaming mug on my nightstand, willing my magic to make it so. I release the magic out into the world and then glance at my nightstand.

Breath rushes out of me in relief. It's there. I touch the side of the mug, and it's damn hot. I may have overdone it a bit, but I stick the tea bag in the mug anyway. It can steep while it cools.

"What's the tea for?" Malcolm's voice almost has me jumping out of my skin. I can't believe I was so engrossed in making a cup of hot water for myself that I forgot he's next to me.

"Kelly said it will help me clear my mind when I fall asleep so it'll be easier to communicate with the goddess."

Malcolm nods. "It's probably best if you supervise. I'm not sure how far under I'll go."

"Of course," Malcolm agrees. "I wouldn't have you do this without me watching over you."

My heart flips and my chest warms. It's nice knowing that I always have someone in my corner. My sisterhood with the ladies aside, having Malcolm there without question is a surprising relief. I know Ayla and the others will always be there for me, but we have divided priorities, and I wouldn't blame them if something had to come before me. With Malcolm, nothing will ever be more important that I am, just as nothing will ever be more important than he is.

We snuggle for a bit before I reach out to test the heat of the tea. It's cool enough to drink now. This is it. I glance at Malcolm with a small smile as I lift the mug. "Bottoms up."

I WAKE up in a beautiful field, the sun a gentle caress against my skin. I blink several times as I look around. Ayla mentioned she'd woken up among some trees, so I expected to do the same.

It is surprisingly calming here, and I feel my spirits lift a bit as I continue to look around. I'm not sure if I need to go searching for Brigid or if she'll come to me. The field stretches out as far as the eye can see, so I linger a bit because the last thing I want to do is get stuck here if I go looking for a goddess.

After waiting a bit longer, I finally decide to start walking, picking a direction at random. I feel more relaxed as I move forward. The sun sinks deliciously into my skin, and a light breeze swirls enticingly around me. Aside from the trees Ayla described, I'm not sure what I expected from this, but it certainly hadn't been the feeling of peace.

"Peace is what you need, my daughter." The light, feminine voice echoes around me. I turn to find the source, but no one is around me. *Weird*. "You hold too much fear, too much anger, and too much anxiety within your soul."

"Well, why don't you come out and talk to me to ease some of that?"

Chapter Seventeen

The laughing goddess who appears before me is not quite what I was expecting either, despite having seen her recently during the vision in Ireland. She's...*more* somehow.

"My daughter," she murmurs, laughter in her tone, "you have never been one to practice patience. It's one of the many things I love about you."

My eyes narrow as I look at her. I'm...not entirely sure what to say to that. She gives me a knowing grin and waves her hand. A table with two cups and two chairs appears.

"Please, take a seat, daughter. We have much to discuss, and my sisters wish to meet you as well."

Well, okay. I guess I'm having a goddess party.

I lower myself slowly into one of the chairs and glance into the cup in front of me. It looks like wine. I raise the glass to my lips and sniff. Merlot. I take a sip and let the wine soak into my tongue before I swallow. It's surprisingly flavorful.

The goddess's laughing eyes meet mine as she watches me enjoy my drink. "I know why you're here, and I will endeavor to give you the answers you seek. I must warn you, however, that there are consequences to seeking some knowledge. It is why we have not provided as much as you would like."

Consequences, huh? Sounds like a load of bullshit to me, but I keep that to myself.

"Okay," I say cautiously. "Can you tell me about the weapons Connor is researching? Are there weapons that can kill the Härja?"

"You know the Härja better as the seven deadly sins." That's...surprising, though I suppose it shouldn't be. "And there are two weapons that can kill them. Connor is right."

"Can you tell us where they are?" The goddess shakes her head. Damn. "Are we expected to kill the Härja or keep them in Hell?"

"The expectation is to stop them however you need to."

Okay. I note she dodged my question about the location of the weapons. "How do we know when a Fate has fallen?" I'm trying to ask the higher priority questions as I remember them.

"Ayla has already fallen," Brigid responds critically. "She has been...tainted."

Tainted? "Care to elaborate?" My tone is a bit more hostile than is probably wise.

"She..." The goddess pauses as though searching for the right words. "Her essence has changed."

She's part demon now. I quirk a brow. That's all it takes?

"But she's still the same person," I argue.

"Is she?"

What the fuck is that supposed to mean?

"I have only one more minute, daughter. There are others who wish to talk to you." She places her hand on mine. "Never stop questioning, and know you will always have my blessing."

With that, she's gone. I'm left sitting alone at the table, staring at the seat she just recently occupied. Ayla isn't the same person? I refuse to believe that. At her core, she is still the same person. Everyone grows, but what makes her fundamentally Ayla hasn't changed.

In the next blink, Coatlicue, the Mother of Gods and Mortals, appears before me. Ayla didn't meet her, and I don't remember seeing her in the vision we had back in Ireland. She's lethally beautiful, with long black hair that shimmers like the night sky and covers her naked breasts, deep brown skin, golden eyes, and a skirt made entirely of snakes.

"Daughter." Her voice is deeper than Brigid's, and it wraps around me like a lover's caress. "I have been warned to avoid punishing you in the manner I wish." I flinch at that. "You have so much doubt in your mind. You have lost your way."

She isn't exactly wrong. I didn't doubt myself or my sisters. I did, however, very much doubt the gods. Everything we've learned so far has me questioning their motives.

"Are we just pawns in a game you're playing with the Härja?" Okay, cool. Good job, Liv. Insult the scary goddess.

She studies me for a moment before she gingerly sits with a weary sigh. "The short answer is no. You are not pawns. When we left your realm for ours and created life on Earth, rules were implemented that needed to be adhered to. The Härja doesn't care to follow those rules. If we don't...the end results will be disastrous."

That has me studying her more closely. It had seemed as though the gods didn't want to get their hands dirty. Which, frankly, pissed me off. But if it's really more complicated than that, if there truly are horrible consequences for their interference, I suppose I'd feel better about us being on the front lines.

"The Härja's intrusion could end not just your realm, but Hell as well. This could lead to the fall of our realm also, but if we interfere too much, it *will* mean the end of your realm." She sighs and glances around the clearing. "You are our children, our hope for a better future. We put pieces of ourselves in you when we created you. We do not want to see all of that destroyed.

"We play by the rules that were established when we created our realm and our children to ensure that not only is the balance maintained, but that life does not simply cease to be."

That...is quite the bombshell. Life just casually stops. Okay. Not good. "I just want to make sure I have this right. Because the gods created their own realm and life, there are rules they can't break, which include helping said life too much, or else things will just...poof? Cease to be?"

"In a nutshell, yes," she confirms.

"I'm not sure how I feel about all of this," I confess.

"There is still much you need to accomplish, and much you have to overcome." She leans over to touch my hand and warmth blossoms in my chest. "We would not have given you this task if we did not believe you wouldn't succeed."

Chapter Eighteen

My body jackknifes into a sitting position, and I suck in a gasping breath. My heart pounds and my head rings.

"Easy, kitten." Malcolm places his hands on my back, and I instantly calm. "Coming out of that sort of meditative sleep can be disorienting."

"You couldn't have mentioned that *before* I went under?" I glare at him over my shoulder. He chuckles and presses a light kiss to my spine. "I think I got some information that can help us. It can wait until the morning though."

"So you were able to connect with Brigid?" I nod. "Good. That's good. Now come snuggle. I promise to keep things strictly PG-13."

That makes me laugh as I settle against him. "I didn't know you were capable of that."

He gasps in mock outrage. "Excuse you, madam, but *you* are the insatiable sexual deviant in this relationship."

An inelegant snort pops out of me. We both know that's a lie.

"Tell me something," I murmur as I snuggle closer to him,

wrapping a leg around his hip. "After all of this is over, do you want to stay here or go back to the UK?"

"I honestly haven't even thought about it, but I don't particularly care so long as you're happy." My heart tumbles slowly in my chest and I can feel a dopey smile forming on my lips. "I do have one demand though."

"A demand, huh?" I arch my brow.

"We need to have at least a dozen babies that all look like you." My eyes water, and I lean in to kiss him.

"I'm surprisingly okay with that." He chuckles against my mouth.

Our kiss quickly becomes heated, and our hands aren't keeping things PG-13 anymore. Malcolm's fingers are just starting to inch under my shirt when I rip away from him, a shocked gasp forcing its way from my lips. "Babies!"

Malcolm slowly pulls away from me, a confused look plastered across his face. "Babies?" He sounds mildly worried.

"Babies!" I yell with excitement and scramble off the bed. I run out of the room and dart to Ayla's, pounding on the door. *Babies!*

An exceptionally grumpy-looking Caleb answers the door. "What's wrong?"

"Is that Liv?" I can hear Ayla farther in the room, so I push my way past Caleb. "What is it?"

I plant myself firmly beside the bed and jab a finger at her. "You're pregnant!"

Her eyes go wide and dart over to Caleb. I can hear Malcolm's shocked inhale. He must have followed me. Ayla's eyes focus back on me before a grin breaks out on her face.

"I didn't want to tell anyone yet. It's still early, and with everything going on—" My squeal of delight cuts her off as I pounce onto the bed, careful not to land on her before I wrap her in my arms.

"I knew there was something going on!" I start peppering

kisses on her cheeks as she laughs and hugs me back. I pull away from Ayla slightly to look at Caleb. "How are you not going full dragon on all our asses?"

He chuckles and crosses his arms over his chest. "It's not easy, trust me, but Ayla puts me in my place...often." He shoots at glare at his mate. "I know I can't keep her from any of this, and frankly, it's driving me insane, but I trust that Ayla will keep herself and our baby safe."

That warms my heart. I know how far Caleb has had to travel to get to this spot. It wasn't easy for either of them—but having a baby! My eyes well with tears and I start sniffling. Malcolm looks at me in panic.

"What's going on?" His voice has a slightly higher pitch to it than normal. "Why is she crying?"

"I'm just so happy." I hug Ayla again.

"Thank you," she says quietly. "I'm worried I won't be able to carry it to term, but I'm going to try. If we haven't finished what we need to before the baby comes, the plan is to keep it here with the community. We know there are a lot of risks" —she shrugs— "but this little one could potentially be a new queen."

I squeeze her one last time before I climb off her bed. My arms wrap around Caleb next. He seems surprised for a moment before he hugs me back.

"We'll do everything we can to keep that little nugget safe. This is the *best* thing to fight for." I smile over at Malcolm as I untangle myself from Caleb and make my way back to my mate. "We promise we won't say anything."

"Thanks." Caleb ushers us out the door. "Get some rest. We'll touch base again in the morning."

We both nod before heading back down the hall to our room.

"You're not going to cry again, are you?" Malcolm sounds like that's the worst thing he can imagine.

"No." I laugh. "But those were happy tears."

"I'm not equipped to handle tears of any variety. It's unsettling." I roll my eyes at him. "It is!"

"Are you sure I'm not the first woman you've been with?" I study him closely as we close the door to our room. "Because if you have *any* experience with women, you know we cry when we're sad, happy, or angry. Sad is sort of self-explanatory. Happy, well, we usually can't really help that, it just sort of bursts out of us..."

"And angry tears?" He's got this weird look on his face as though he isn't sure if he should sit down or run.

"When we cry when we're angry, it's because murder is illegal," I deadpan. "We usually visualize killing men in different manners, and we get extremely upset that we can't actually enact any of those scenarios."

"Good to know..." Malcolm drawls slowly. "Have you, uh, thought about killing me?"

"Almost daily," I chirp happily.

After breakfast the next morning, we all remain sitting around the table. Everyone seems eager to hear about whether the tea worked. I'm slightly worried I didn't get enough information before I woke up.

"It worked," I start. "I was able to meet with Brigid and Coatlicue." I relay all of the information I was able to gain. I try to break the news about Ayla being "tainted" as gently as possible, but she still flinches like I slapped her.

"Hey!" My voice is sharp. "None of that. You know none of us here think anything like that."

"I know, but the transition has been difficult. I'm a bit more bloodthirsty than I was before." Caleb leans over to wrap an arm around her. "Sometimes I'm a lot angrier than I should be." She sighs and runs her fingers through her hair.

"We're all here for you," Darcy soothes. "Without you, none of this would be possible. You're our center. We won't let you stray."

I can feel Ayla's happiness warm and bright through the bond.

Connor stands. "I think I have a few locations we can try. Let me double-check." He rushes off.

"We should get ready. Who knows how long this will actually take." Caleb gets to his feet. "I think it's best if we all go this time. We'll leave competent people in charge while we're away, but we might need all hands on deck for this."

We nod. It hits me then that in less than a year, my life has gone from living under a sketchy as fuck alpha with other shifters to a world that is so much bigger and far more complex than I ever imagined possible. I have powers I'm only just beginning to understand, a mate who has very little problem banging my brains out in front of other people, and I've met two goddesses.

Life has gotten weird.

"You ready to get packing?" Malcolm leans in to press a kiss to my temple. I smile at him and nod.

I don't need to take much, regardless of how long we are gone. Magic is certainly a perk when it comes to cleaning clothes and doing general housework, but Connor didn't exactly give us any idea of where we need to trek off to, so I want to be semi-prepared for different climates. Thankfully, I'm able to keep everything to a single backpack.

"I don't think I've ever seen another female able to pack as light as that," Malcolm comments, sounding impressed. I raise my brow with a huff. "What? Most women pack about a year's worth of stuff for a weekend away. Tell me I'm wrong."

"You aren't," I concede. "But *most* women don't have magic."

"Even the ones who do."

I roll my eyes at him, *pendejo*. "Let's just get out front."

"After you, kitten." He holds the door open, letting me lead us down the hall to the front door.

Unlike our trip to Ireland, it looks like just our core group is heading off to hunt down these sin slaying weapons. Which, frankly, is probably a good thing. We don't want to draw too much attention to ourselves, and if someone is watching us, having a large group will do just that.

Ripley and Xin are here to see us off. I'm mildly surprised at how fast the young witch has integrated herself into our inner circle, but that's not a bad thing. We need more people to step up when our core can't be around. Ayla is talking animatedly with them, so I make my way over.

"Is everything all set?" I glance between Ayla and the others.

"All good! I was just seeing how things were going with the blood bank. I had Xin make the announcement since we're not off on an epic side quest." Epic side quest indeed.

"Everything is going smoothly, and I can handle getting donations set up," Ripley says with a bright smile. How is she able to be so damn perky?

"Dante and Darcy were given some of the supernatural supply we were already able to collect." Xin bows his head in the direction of the other two vampires. "I am sure they will need it."

"Thank you for thinking of that." I'm mildly miffed that I didn't.

"Let's get this show on the road!" Darcy's shout has all of us turning in her direction. Kelly already has a portal set up to the coordinates Connor gave her, and it looks as though they're just waiting on us to head out. "If I could die of old age, I would have by now!"

I snort. So dramatic.

With a wave, Ayla and I head toward the group as they all start to file through the portal. I'm uneasy about not knowing where exactly we're going, but I trust Connor.

WE STEP out of the portal onto what looks like an old lava field. Taking a deep inhale to pull in the local scents, I allow the fresh, nearly unspoiled air to inflate my lungs. Wherever we are, there's certainly not as much pollution as there is back home.

"Welcome to Iceland," Connor announces with his arms spread wide.

Summer in Iceland means the sun isn't ever going to set below the horizon. I've never been, but I've heard so many good things about this still slightly untamed country. I make a note to ensure Malcolm and I come back. This place just feels...right.

"Okay, Captain, where the hell in Iceland are we?" Malcolm looks around, taking in the lava fields and the mountains in the distance. "And where do we need to end up?"

"We're on the Holuhraun lava field," Connor explains. "It's the closest I could get us to our final destination. Portaling onto a glacier isn't advised. We need to make it to the Vatnajökull ice cap."

"I'm not even going to try to say what you just said," I mumble. "Okay, so we need to get to the ice cap?"

"Well, technically we need to get *beneath* the ice cap." Connor rubs the back of his neck when we all whirl to face him. "There are several volcanoes beneath the ice cap. Typically, ice caves form in the winter due to the melts in the spring and summer."

"I realize I may be a bit slow here, but how the *hell* are we getting beneath all that ice. Into a volcano?" Malcolm runs his fingers through his hair and adjusts his glasses, looking very frazzled and delicious. Deliciously frazzled.

"Well, that's going to be the hard part," Connor admits. "I think we should talk while we're hiking. Even though the sun doesn't set this time of year, we're still going to have to camp out on the glacier for at least one night before we find the right spot."

"And how do you know when we've found the right spot?" I ask as we all start trudging along the lava field, dutifully following behind Connor.

"That's the hard part." My mind stutters a bit. That is going to be the hard part? What the hell had Connor gotten us into? "The texts weren't entirely clear on that aspect, but I was able to find a reference to the Fates and the weapons, so I think Ayla should be able to feel it once we get close."

I blink.

We're hiking across lava fields and over and through an ice cap on the hopes that Ayla will *feel* something when we get close? Insert Lego Batman once again. Let's also throw in a solid Yzma from the *Emperor's New Groove* here too. Why me?

This is going to be great. I can just feel it.

Chapter Nineteen

We stop on the edge of the ice cap to make camp. Connor isn't entirely sure how long it'll take for us to find where we need to be, and this ice cap is *huge*. Apparently, the thing takes up roughly eight percent of the entire country. So…this is going to be loads of fun.

Fayden had given me *Abuela's* journal after our initial meeting, since she'd already put all of the information into her A.I. I brought it along, figuring it wouldn't hurt to skim through it. I'm glad I did. It rests on my thighs, and while I want to dig in, I'm mildly nervous about what I'll find.

Malcolm and I are sitting close to the fire, the others forming a circle on either side of us. The chatter has died down, and we're all off in our own little worlds. I think what we're doing and the fact that we're just hoping we'll stumble across an area where Ayla's Fate senses tingle has finally sunk in for all of us.

I glance across the fire at Kelly, tapping into our bond just to see how she's holding up. She's been pretty closed off lately, which is understandable, but I'm worried about her. I can't pick up much, but she seems to be fairly mellow right now, which is good. She has dark circles under her eyes, though, and she's still too damn thin for my liking. The pack animal in me wants to scoop her up, feed her all the cookies, and just snarl at all the people who made her sad. No one hurts pack.

"What does *Abuela's* journal say?" Darcy asks, drawing my attention to her. We haven't spent much time together since she joined our group, but it still feels as though she's been with us all along.

"Yeah," Dante chimes in. "We might as well hear about her adventures while we've got some down time."

My lips twitch. Knowing *Abuela*, searching for information on the prophecy was certainly an adventure. I won't be surprised if she mentions beating someone for information... or apparently sleeping with them. Like ya do.

Malcolm rests his hand on the small of my back, and I shoot him a small smile. The touch centers me. I crack open the journal, the scent of worn leather and old parchment filling the air as I do. I inhale deeply because I love that scent. Books.

"There's no date," I start, "but the first entry talks about tracking down a few witch families who were famous for their oracles." I skim the page before I start to read.

I am in London, trying to find one of the oldest known oracle families. From what I have been able to gather from my talks with others, their line goes back to Babylon. They claim they are directly related to Apollo. Their matriarch, Mary, wishes to meet at the Globe for a production of a new play called Macbeth. *Apparently, one of her coven mates wrote the play, and she insists it's a masterpiece—as though we have time for such nonsense.*

But Mary may have some of the answers I seek.

I met with Mary and sat through her "masterpiece." It was decent, but certainly not to the caliber I'm used to back home. When I told her the specific prophecy I was seeking information about, she became oddly subdued. I could see she knew something, and luckily for her, she didn't attempt to hide it.

She confirmed the first known written record of the prophecy dates to the fall of the Roman Empire. It was recorded by a Roman oracle not of her line. She insists that line has died out, but I will see.

Mary also claimed the prophecy changed over time, which is odd. Prophecies, true prophecies given by the gods, do not change. But this one is famous. Mary does not know the original prophecy and cannot tell me anything aside from the Roman oracle's family name—Caesar. I will have to see if what she says is true, but someone has to know more.

The pop and crackle of the fire seems to scream into the night when I finish the entry. Shakespeare was a witch? And Caesar...as in Julius Caesar? There are so many implications, and the fact that my *Abuela* didn't already know who these people were... Well, of course she wouldn't have known. If she saw an original production of *Macbeth*, it would have been the early 1600s. Since she'd never really been outside of our pack territory, she wouldn't have known who Julius Caesar was. She also wouldn't have known who Shakespeare was.

"So I think it bears repeating," Ayla murmurs, her amused tone floating over the crackling fire, "your *Abuela* is badass." We all chuckle. "Care to read another? Then we can talk about it, dissect it, and then go to sleep on this nice hunk of lava."

I arch a brow at her. "Sure."

I have been able to track down a Caesar descendent. I agreed to a blood oath not to reveal this person's name, not even within this journal. They confirmed the Roman oracle was not the first to produce the prophecy. They also stated that it has been passed down that the original prophecy did not come from the gods. It came from a much darker source. It was originally much more horrific, suggesting there was no way to prevent the gates of Hell from opening, no way to stop the monsters from getting out, and no way to once again seal the gates.

The version Aine gave to my Ximena is the version foretold from her ancestor. It was given to her by Athena. They were forbidden from writing the interaction down, and thus everything they know of it has passed orally. The only thing the oracle could record was the prophecy itself.

The Caesar tells me Athena risked much in changing the original prophecy, but they believe it was to ensure that our world could survive if it ever came to pass. Their line has not been blessed with a prophecy since.

I blow out a breath. "I'm going to go out on a limb and say the original, darker source of the prophecy was one of the Härja." Everyone nods. "And based on my own conversation with Brigid, Athena really did risk a lot by changing the prophecy to give us a fighting chance."

"Based on your experience, I'd agree," Connor rumbles. "But frankly, I'm not sure how the history of the prophecy is relevant at this point." He shrugs. "I could be missing something. My brain is pretty wrapped up in the weapons right now."

"It helps to reinforce what Brigid told Liv," Malcolm reasons. "If anything, it means they aren't playing us. We could take the gods at their word, but when has that really ever worked out for anyone? Having a history of the prophecy will help us understand what we're supposed to do, when, and whether we can trust the information we've been given by the gods."

I close the journal and hug it to my chest. I'll keep sharing the entries as we continue our little Iceland side quest. There are answers in here, we already know that, but it's also possible we're missing clues and helpful hints. We didn't exactly get a chance to dive into everything with Fayden before we took off.

"I'm going to get some sleep." Ayla yawns, standing and

stretching before heading off to her tent. Caleb follows closely behind her.

"Good idea." Malcolm nudges me, and we head off to our tent. The others, with the exception of Darcy and Dante, do the same.

≈

MALCOLM HAD to put a spell on our tent so I could actually sleep last night. The fact that the sun doesn't set here during the summer months threw me off completely, so I'm groggy and cranky in the morning. I can hear some of the others already up and moving around camp, Malcolm among them. Meanwhile, I'm sprawled out on the air mattress, trying to find the will to live.

Wasn't it morning yesterday? Why does it have to be morning again? Especially when there was no night.

Malcolm steps up to the tent and peeks in through the mesh door. "You doing okay in there, kitten?"

"Yeah, totally fine."

"I have coffee for you." This perks me up. "Why don't you get dressed and come get it? We're almost done making breakfast."

I grumble my acceptance of his terms and toss on some clothes. Out at the fire pit, where Kelly is making something that smells amazing, I snag my coffee and park my butt by the fire.

"Do you even have a general direction we should be walking in?" Ayla asks Connor. "My Fate senses aren't tingling, and I'm not feeling pulled anywhere. At least not right now."

"I figured the best bet would be to head toward the middle of the ice cap, you should pick something up along the way." I kind of want to bitch slap the dire wolf. This is the most half-assed side quest ever.

Darcy and Dante each have a bag of blood against their mouths as their eyes narrow on Connor. Seems like I'm not the only one who's annoyed with the overgrown dog. I fight to suppress my smirk. We don't want any infighting, but I can't help the urge to give him just a bit of a hard time.

"So we just aimlessly wander on a giant hunk of ice over active volcanoes and just wait for some tingles?" I don't even bother to try to tone down the sass. "Just so I'm getting this right."

Connor narrows his eyes on me and looks to Malcolm.

"Oh, honey, no. He can't help you." I chuckle when his gaze swings back to me. "He knows better than to try."

"She's not wrong, Con." Malcolm chuckles and moves to stand behind me, out of firing range.

"Look, I know this isn't exactly...ideal. But it's the best I have. We can't go after Ayla's sisters without also having these weapons." He's right, but I don't care to admit it.

"Maybe if the four of us" —Kelly gestures at herself, Ayla, Darcy, and me— "attempt to link up, we might be able to give Ayla a power boost to feel where the weapon is."

"It's not a terrible idea," Malcolm mutters. "Even without you and Darcy technically being queens yet, you're both very powerful, and the four of you are linked in a way the rest of us aren't. It can't hurt."

"Let's do this." Ayla seems pumped to give it a shot. Someone has had her morning cup of coffee.

I down mine as Kelly instructs Connor on how to finish breakfast. Then we're all standing together away from the fire with Malcolm and Connor there to watch over us.

"Here." Kelly hands out the charms that were in the box at Ayla's cottage in Ireland. "Let's hold onto these. They might help." I hadn't realized she ended up with them.

We all clasp hands and take a few fortifying breaths. I relax my muscles and close my eyes. The moment we all lower our shields, power rushes through us. It's warm and familiar, playful almost with its enthusiasm to heed our call.

We gently push the energy into Ayla, who then gives it a specific task. And boy, does it seek and destroy. A map appears in my mind and a pulse of blue light bursts out from where we are, then a small red dot appears as our combined magic washes over what I very much hope is the weapon.

"I think that's it," Ayla breathes. "I think we found it!"

We allow our magic to taper off and we drop our hands. My eyes flutter open, and I notice everyone is smiling. I can still see that ping of red, and now I can also feel a slight tug in my center leading me to it. Finally, a break.

"I think we can all feel it," I say, and the others nod. "This is great. Much better than aimlessly wandering a giant chunk of ice."

Breaking down camp goes faster than setting it up. Everyone's excitement is palpable. It'll still take us a while, maybe a day or more, to get to where that magical ping is, but it's more like a solid mission now than it was even a few moments ago.

We head out across the ice cape with a bit of pep in our steps. Having a clear sense of where we need to be reassures all of us, and we're able to move at a fast clip. We should only need to spend one night on the ice at this rate—unless we can't get under the ice, that is.

That's something that still bothers me. Once we get there, how the hell are we supposed to get to the weapon?

"Hey, kitten," Malcolm murmurs as he links his arm with mine. "I can practically hear you thinking. What's going on in that beautiful head of yours?"

"Just curious about how we're going to get under the ice

to get to this weapon. We don't even know what the weapon is. Is it some sort of sword? Is it some form of magic?"

Malcolm chuckles and tugs me to a stop, letting the rest of our group move ahead of us. "I think you need to slow that brain of yours down a bit. I know you're used to thinking up as many different scenarios as you can, but let's try to take this particular adventure one step at a time. We're learning new information as we go, so there's really no need to try to micromanage every detail."

He's right. "That's easier said than done," I grumble.

"I know it is." He smiles and leans down to press a quick kiss to my lips. "But you have a mate to help you take your mind off things and assist with your troubles."

I grin up at him. "Awfully helpful."

"I do what I can, kitten."

"I may need your help with something later." I nudge us into moving again, not wanting the rest of our group to get too far ahead.

"Oh?" His eyes light up and a knowing grin spreads across his face. "And what might that be?"

"It's a very serious need."

"I see." Malcom's face smooths out.

"I haven't had any orgasms lately. You've been slacking in your main duty as my mate." I throw a mock glare in his direction, only to see his lips twitch as he fights a smirk.

"I understand." He places a hand over his heart. "I will endeavor to make sure you come at least five times a day."

"I suppose that's sufficient," I giggle.

"Only the best orgasms for you, kitten." His voice, dark and smooth, curls around me, causing me to shiver slightly. "Should I tell you what I want to do to you in the meantime?"

I shudder at the thought. I'm turned on by the idea and mildly terrified. Do I really want to risk the others over-hearing Malcolm talking dirty to me?

Taking my silence as permission, Malcolm begins, "I can't wait to lick that delicious pussy of yours again. I love watching you squirm and moan against my tongue. You get even more lively when I slide my fingers into you."

I feel my face heat as a blush creeps over my cheeks and heat pools between my legs. Ayla's amusement trickles down the pack bond. Everyone can hear him, which means... everyone can hear me. An evil smile curls my lips. Two can play at this game.

Chapter Twenty

I bat my eyes as I turn to face Malcolm. If this is how he wants to play the mate game, then game on. I unlink our arms so I can slide an arm up his chest, plastering myself against him as we walk.

"I think instead of you licking me, I should be the one licking you." I keep my voice low and husky. "I'd run my tongue along the tip as I cup your balls with one hand and the base of your cock with the other." I slide my hand down his chest to rub his hardening cock. "You know how much I love to tease you, so I won't take you in my mouth. I'll lightly run my tongue up and down your length."

Malcolm's hand connects with my ass, causing me to jump with a slight yelp. "That's enough of that, kitten."

"You're the one who started this, so if you can't take the heat..." I trail off with a grin. His gaze whips to connect with mine. With narrowed eyes, he stops and pulls me flush against his chest. As his lips crash against mine, I hear a low growl come from him, which prompts my panther to purr in response.

Our mouths battle for dominance, each of us nipping and

licking at the other. My fingers thread into his hair. One of his hands tangles in my braid while the other grasps my ass to grind me against his erection. I fist my hands in his hair, trying to drag him closer.

A loud cough sounds from behind us, and for a moment, we don't process that we're holding up the group. We continue to maul each other, but another loud cough has us slowly breaking apart, and Malcolm gently takes my lower lip between his teeth as he goes.

"As much as we'd all enjoy the show," Dante comments with a chuckle, "we need to keep going if we're going to get to our destination by tomorrow."

I let out a dramatic groan as I pull myself away from my mate. This whole saving the world bullshit is such a cock-block. Clam jam?

"I'll make sure to soundproof all of our tents tonight," Kelly adds helpfully. I shoot her a broad grin and some finger guns. Wing woman of the year right there. The others groan loudly, and then they groan again when Ayla holds both her hands up to insert her forefinger into the hole made by the fingers of her other hand. Crude. I laugh.

We all start moving again, and Malcolm and I catch up to the group. He's got a look on his face that tells me he's plotting something, and I'm not entirely sure I want to know what it is. A girl likes surprises, especially of the sexual variety.

≈

WE MAKE it to the halfway point before stopping for the night. Thankfully with Ayla, Kelly, and Malcolm, we're able to make sure the tents stay toasty all night, and they are all now soundproof. Malcolm walks me through the spell, and I get our tent all settled on my own, which is fairly exciting.

Instead of staring blankly at the fire, Ayla and I move away from the main camp. She's going to continue my flying lessons. Caleb watches from a distance, ready to shout instructions as needed. We both strip out of our clothes and shift. I allow my panther to take a moment to bask in being free. She stretches in that way only a purely satisfied cat can and expands her wings.

I feel like I'm going to need to have a running leap.

Ayla laughs through our bond. *Watch how I move. I can't go too slow or I won't get off the ground, but I'm going to show you all the parts and then take off.*

I nod, staring intently at the dragon in front of me.

In exaggerated movements that would normally have me laughing, Ayla stretches her wings out. Her body coils, and tension ripples through every muscle from holding the position for me to study. She launches herself into the air, her wings tucking close to her body as she shoots up before snapping out to begin flapping.

"The magic helps with flying," Caleb remarks. "For regular dragons, it's the innate magic of our shifter genes. For queens, there's also that hint of magic that should help you. Just... don't think too hard about it."

I turn to shoot him my best cat glare. I can do this. My back legs knead a bit in anticipation. I got this.

Copying all of the motions Ayla showed me, I launch myself into the air with every ounce of power I possess. My wings start beating when I hit the pinnacle of my leap. The feeling of weightlessness is amazing, and the air rushing through my fur is similar to what I feel when I'm running through the forest.

I land with a jarring thud that vibrates my entire spine before I fly onto my back with my wings spread. My legs claw helplessly at the air as I try to roll myself over, looking very much like a turtle stuck on its back. The wings are the main issue. They are not moving in a way that will be of any use in getting me upright again. My panther panics the longer we're on our back and exposing our very vulnerable, soft belly.

Caleb's loud burst of laughter and the sensation of Ayla's amusement has me shifting back to my human form quickly before once again changing into my panther. I will have my revenge.

I realize your panther has never flown before, but I suggest you trust her to take over for a bit. Thinking too much is detrimental to learning how to fly. Ayla's laughing tone has me flinging a glare at her.

I gently nudge my panther, allowing her to shift to the forefront of our mind. She feels far more confident about all of this than I do. I'm not sure if that's reassuring or alarming, but it's time to nut up or shut up.

She takes a few moments to pace a bit, getting a better feel for her wings before she launches herself into the air. She keeps going, her wings pumping hard to shoot us higher than Ayla. A loud whoop of excitement comes from our mate on the ground, and a sense of pleased pride fills us. The others are all cheering me on as I level out and start zooming around.

Ayla comes to fly beside me, her dragon taunting my panther into a game of tag. We play for a bit before landing. My back is sore, the muscles not quite used to the strain of keeping the wings moving and our body in the air. We shift back and quickly dress.

I high-five a grinning Caleb as we all make our way toward the glowing campfire. I'm still going to need to practice, but at least I know I can get off the ground if I need to.

Malcolm wraps his arms around my shoulders as I settle in next to him. I feel his pride through our bond, and I give him a bright smile. Someone is getting lucky tonight. With that thought in mind, I stand and pull him up and over to our tent. I can hear a few knowing chuckles from the men in our group, but I ignore them.

"Give it to her good, witch!" Ayla shouts. Both of us groan, not bothering to respond as we zip up the tent and shut the rest of the world out.

Thankfully, because of magic, the tent is actually bigger on the inside. I will admit that I love me a TARDIS tent. We're able to stand comfortably, and we even have a large air mattress. There's a soft glow that's coming from seemingly nowhere, and with the snap of my fingers, it'll go out. Magic is boss.

Malcolm looks me over with something shining in his eyes that makes me feel all warm and fuzzy. He's proud of me and he loves me. It's all there, written across his face. I can also feel it thrumming down the bond, hot and steady, anchoring me in place. I do my best to shove my love in his direction, keeping my face open so he can see it written there too.

Slowly, as though he has all the time in the world, Malcolm brings his face close to mine. I'm not quite so leisurely, so I push up on my tiptoes to wrap my arms around his neck and firmly plant my lips against his. He smiles against my lips as he returns the kiss.

Malcolm's lips are firm with a silky texture I want to get lost in for days. I'm pretty sure I could spend the rest of our lives kissing him and be happy. Our tongues play, swirling and licking, and we nibble on each other's lips. I release a happy sigh. He grips my waist and holds me against him.

He pulls back a bit and rests his forehead against mine. "No matter what happens tomorrow, you've come so damn far, and I couldn't be more proud to have you as my mate."

My chocolate brown eyes gaze into his and a smile curves my lips. "Are you getting sentimental on me?"

His expression is serious as he responds, "We have no idea what's going to happen when we make it to the weapon. I want to make sure there's no doubt in your mind when it comes to how I feel about you."

I lift my hands to gently cup his face, my eyes searching his. "Don't make this seem like goodbye. I've claimed you, there are no take backs. There's no way we won't get out of this together."

Malcolm nods before kissing me again. This time the kiss is filled with hunger. This isn't a sweet kiss meant to convey love or affection. No. This kiss is meant to claim, dominate, and mark. He wants to make sure that not only do I know the softer feelings he has for me, but the primal ones too. I'm more than happy to reciprocate.

He starts to slowly peel my clothes off instead of magicking them away. This is nice. It builds the anticipation. Not to mention, I get to feel his hands all over me.

Not to be outdone, I start to drag his clothes off him. Our lips only part to remove our shirts. Once that's out of the way, we fuse them together again. There's a different kind of edge to us tonight. It's not overtly urgent, but it certainly isn't slow either.

Regardless of what it is, I know I just want his hands on me and to feel his cock slide within me to the hilt over and over again. I want to tangle my hands in his hair and blur the lines of where I end and he begins. I want everything he has to give me. Everything.

Malcolm lifts me, walks me over to our bed, and then gently places me down. He stands there looking at me for a moment, his face etched with hunger and his eyes shining with love. I'm not sure I'll ever really get used to seeing that look on his face. It takes my breath away and leaves me tingling and aching to be touched.

The soft glide of his fingertips up my leg has me releasing a shudder of anticipation. I don't want to rush this, but I also don't want him to take forever either, so I decide to take matters into my own hands.

Gripping his shoulders, I use my shifter strength and speed to switch us so he's on his back and I'm straddling him. A deep rumble starts in his chest, and his lips stretch into a roguish grin.

"Are you planning on sliding that wet, hot little pussy down on my cock, kitten?" His hands grip my hips, and he grinds my clit against his cock. I have to bite back a moan. "Are you going to impale yourself and then use me for your own pleasure?"

"Damn straight. That's exactly what I'm going to do." I wink at him then grind down against him again.

"Don't get too cocky, kitten. You're going to beg me to fill that pussy up with my come. It's going to overflow your channel and slide down those deliciously juicy thighs. Then you're going to ask me for more."

"You know what?" I lean down so our lips brush when I speak. "That's exactly what I want."

I reach down and line his cock up with my entrance. I lower my hips as my pussy slides along his dick. I don't need any foreplay tonight, just looking at him is enough to leave me painfully aroused. When my hips are flush with his, I press a gentle kiss to his lips before sitting upright. I lean back and plant my hands on his thighs.

"I want you to watch my pussy as it eats your cock, witch." I clench down around him, and he lets out a soft grunt. "Then you can watch your come drip from me and down your cock to your balls. Are you ready?"

"I love it when you talk dirty, kitten." I blush.

He nods. My hips rise only slightly before I'm moving back down. One of his hands helps keep me steady while the other one quickly works my nipples until they are aching peaks. He then allows his magic to take over teasing them so his hand can gently, softly, flick my clit. Malcolm does it as I glide up and sink down.

I let my head fall back and my eyes close as waves of pleasure crash within me, focusing on the feeling. We keep a steady, even pace, both of us moaning ever so often. I love hearing him when he's inside me. I love knowing I'm the one who makes him feel like this.

"I need to feel your pussy flutter around my cock, kitten. I want it gripping me tight and demanding I fill it up."

I compress around him, making sure to keep clenching as I pick up my pace.

A quietly muttered, "Fuck," brings me closer to the edge. My chest is heaving, and all I can focus on is the feel of him inside me, hitting me in every delicious spot, even the ones I didn't know I had before him. His finger presses more firmly against my clit, causing me to cry out.

"Come all over my cock, kitten. Do it now." At his firm command, I shatter, screaming his name as I drown in an ocean of pleasure.

He groans as he meets his own end, but it appears that this isn't enough to satisfy my witch. He sits up, wrapping his arms tightly around me. Gently removing himself from my body, Malcolm then moves to stand at the edge of the bed. With sure actions, he adjusts me on my hands and knees in front of him.

"Fuck." He runs his finger along my slit before he presses against me from behind, bringing his finger up in front of my face. "Look at that, kitten."

His finger is glistening with not only his come but mine as well. Malcolm presses his finger against my mouth, and I eagerly open for him, flicking my tongue out to clean the digit.

Slap!

I moan around his finger at the sting of his palm connecting with my flesh.

Slap!

Malcolm's finger slides out of my mouth as I turn my head to look back at him. He's grinning from ear to ear. I shiver. It's not a friendly grin. This is the grin of a predator, and I'm most definitely his prey.

He smooths his hand over the curve of my ass, easing the sting of his slaps. My eyes widen when I see he's already hard again. I knew my witch was insatiable and had impressive stamina, but this is a new record for him. My tongue darts out, and I drag it suggestively along my lower lip. His eyes track the movement before lifting to meet my gaze.

"Remember, kitten. You said you wanted to be so full of my come that it would drip down your thighs. That means you're not going to be getting a lot of sleep tonight." His voice is a dark, delicious promise.

"Don't tease me, witch."

He chuckles, lining his cock up with my entrance. I keep my head in a position that allows me to gaze directly into his eyes. They never once wander as he slowly, so fucking slowly, sinks into me. My eyelids flutter, and I release a low moan.

"I love how wet you get for me, kitten." Malcolm's grin is wicked. He bends down to press a kiss to my spine before slowly dragging his cock back in a way that hits every damn nerve ending.

I can't keep my head at this angle, so I rest it against the bed and let my hands tangle in the sheets above me. When he slides in again, he does it with such force that I need to press down to keep myself from slipping forward. I widen my legs a bit more and purr as he slides back out. This angle is perfect. So wonderfully perfect. I can feel everything.

"Slam your thick cock into me, mate. Make me scream." The purr in my words has his hands gripping my hips tighter.

"Challenge accepted, kitten." With that, he starts an even rhythm. Each time he thrusts in, he goes as deep as possible, making sure to add enough force at the end to have me clinging onto the sheets to stay in place.

My gasp fills the space around us when I feel one of his fingers nudge against my ass. It slips in just a bit, and it adds to my pleasure. We haven't exactly had the anal talk, but I'm not opposed.

My thoughts scatter as his magic starts a rough, unrelenting thrum against my clit. I can hear my cries echo around us. I'm begging him for more, to go harder, faster. I want it all.

"Make me come, Malcolm," I whimper. "I want to come around your cock again."

"Good girl, kitten," he grinds out. He's just as close as I am.

His finger slides deeper into me at the same time he thrusts firmly inside me and his magic sharply pinches my clit. It's a stimulation overload that throws me off the damn cliff and has me free falling.

I'm not sure how long I come. I'm pretty sure this is the longest, most intense orgasm I've ever had. Can an orgasm kill you? Because if this keeps going, I'm certain my heart is going to give out. I collapse onto the bed, my pussy still fluttering from the aftershocks, my legs shaking slightly.

I almost don't feel Malcolm cleaning me with a damp cloth. I also miss the feeling of his lips as they drag along my body as he cleans me.

"I'll give you five minutes, kitten. Then I'm going to fuck you until you can't see straight."

I'm really okay with that. Sounds like a good plan.

Chapter Twenty-One

All during the next day, my mind keeps replaying last night. Malcolm hadn't been lying when he said I wasn't going to get much sleep, and he sure as fuck hadn't lied about fucking me until I couldn't see straight. He pretty much fucked me into a damn coma. My body is sore and aching in all the right places. I'm surprisingly still turned on too. Gods, this witch is going to turn me into some sort of sex addict.

When we finally arrive at the spot where we'd felt the pulse of magic indicating the weapon, there isn't much to see. There is just miles and miles of ice. Sure, it is pretty ice, but it's still just ice. I crouch to tap a finger on the hard surface. It's not just white here, there are gorgeous blues and blacks mixed in. With the next tap of my finger, I send some of my magic down into the ice, using it as a sonar. Kelly, Ayla, and Malcolm all squat to do the same.

I don't feel anything as my magic penetrates the almost four miles of ice beneath my feet. I push a little harder so it can search through the hardened magma below. It takes a while, but I eventually feel my magic connect with the energy around the weapon. The image it casts in my mind has me believing that it's a long, curved sword. I'm interested to see if I'm right.

I flick my gaze up to the other three around me. As one, they all look up and meet my eyes. "Did you guys meet the magic down in the volcano?" They nod. "Did it feel like a curved sword?"

"Yeah," Kelly answers with a thoughtful look on her face. "I've never had my magic tell me the shape of an item before. When I've done magic like this in the past, it always came back as a blob."

Malcolm nods his agreement.

"So we need to get through four miles of ice and roughly one mile of hardened magma." Ayla stands, and so do the rest of us. She starts pacing and runs a hand through her hair as she thinks. "Did anyone feel if the volcano is currently active?"

"According to the website," Connor replies, drawing our eyes to him as he scrolls on his phone, "the volcanos here are active, though the threat of an eruption is minimal. It looks like the volcanoes erupt every one hundred to one hundred fifty years. The last eruption was just a few years ago."

Everyone seems to sag with relief. At least that's something we don't need to worry about. I just wish it was more reassuring.

"How are we going to do this?" I ask.

"I can hold the ice open," Kelly volunteers. "I'd need someone to open the volcano, but I can hold the ice."

"I'll hold the volcano. It felt like it was in a cave system, and I doubt it'll be as easy as magically opening a tunnel to it, so I'll open it a bit off from the chamber where the weapon is." Ayla looks at the rest of us. "Caleb and Connor will stay up here with us in case anyone shows up. I think Dante should stay up here too."

Dante nods. Darcy moves over to stand next to me.

"Alright, I guess you two are with me." I smile at Darcy and Malcolm.

"Ready?" Kelly inquires.

We all nod, and she takes a deep breath before holding her hands out, her palms facing the ice. The ground beneath us starts to rumble and tremble softly. She grunts quietly and then moves her hands to her sides as a wide hole opens in the ice.

Ayla steps up next to Kelly and mirrors her actions. I can sense their focus down the bond, which means we should get in and out as quickly as possible. Malcolm can sense it too, so he ushers us to the edge of the hole and we all glance down. Damn.

"I'm going to have my magic padded around us. Don't worry about the fall," Malcolm murmurs in reassurance. He grabs both of our hands, and we jump.

WE FALL for what feels like forever. I hadn't ever had a reason to think about how long it would take to plunge five miles. Now I know—forever. I have no idea how high skydivers are when they jump out of planes, I've never had an interest in something like that, but if it's anything like this, you have a lot of time to think about life...and death.

"Are you *sure* you are going to be able to slow us down enough for us not to splat like bugs at the bottom?" I ask. "Not that I don't trust you or your magic, but this is a really long way to fall."

Malcolm chuckles and leans in to kiss my temple. "Are you afraid of heights, kitten? You're a flying panther."

"Hey now." I lift my finger in his face. "I've only just become a flying panther, and cats aren't supposed to fly!" This time Darcy joins Malcolm as they laugh. I toss them both a withering glare before fixing my gaze forward.

"Don't worry, kitten. We're completely safe."

"Uh-huh, sure." I stick my tongue out at him. He grins at me.

A few silent moments later, I can feel us slowing. I glance down, a little relieved to see that the ground isn't rushing at us in a way that suggests imminent death. I can scratch off dying like a bug on a windshield off my list of things to worry about.

Once our feet are firmly planted on solid ground again, we look around. There are numerous passages that sprawl away from the tunnel. The pull to the weapon is coming from our left so we head that way.

Before Malcolm can do it, a fireball appears in my hand to illuminate the caverns around us. No. Not caverns. Lava tubes. And they are huge. We all look around in wonder. This place is amazing and, admittedly, creepy.

We come to a dead end, and I cock my head. This is the right tunnel. I can feel it. So why the hell does it just cut off like that? While Darcy and Malcolm begin feeling the walls around us in case we missed a small turn off, I close my eyes and let my magic ease out of me.

Well fuck me sideways with a cactus.

"Don't touch anything." My voice whips out of me with so much force the other two still. "We need to be careful."

"What do you feel?" Malcolm comes over as my eyes slide open. He looks confused and curious. "I can't feel anything."

"Neither can I," Darcy mutters as she stands beside Malcolm.

"This place is booby-trapped to high heaven. We need to go through that wall." I point to the wall directly in front of me. "But if we do, all sorts of unpleasant things will trigger. We might actually cause an eruption."

Which, frankly, is not the way I want to die. The way the magic in here feels tells me it would be a slow and exceptionally painful death. I like living. A lot. Team not death, anyone?

"What if we don't use magic to get through the wall?" Darcy questions. "I'm strong enough that I can dig through this fairly quickly."

I'm...not sure. I take a step closer to the wall, causing Malcolm to stiffen in alarm. I wave him back before I gently place my hand on the rock surface. Instead of pushing my magic out of me, I try to pull the magic surrounding the weapon into me so I can read it.

I'm blown pretty far down the tunnel, landing on my back with a loud thud and a soft grunt. The back of my head cracks against the floor. Ow, motherfucker, that hurt. Malcolm shouts and rushes after me. He kneels beside me, wrapping his large hand behind my neck to help me sit up. I press my fingers against my temples and groan.

"I feel like I've been run over by a Mack truck." My pulse pounds in my eyes and skull. A sense of nausea rolls through me, and I need to take a few deep breaths to get through it. Whatever magic is protecting that weapon, it does not want anything to get to the blade.

"Olivia." Malcolm's voice is firm and full of concern. "Look at me, kitten."

My gaze swings to his and he curses. "I think you have a concussion. Your pupils are huge. How does your head feel?"

"Like it's about to split open and ooze my brains out all over the ground."

"Fuck. Darcy!" The vampire comes to my other side. "She's most likely got a pretty bad concussion. I don't want to ask you to do this—"

"I'll try to dig into the wall, but you need to be ready to

run, Malcolm." They study each other for a minute before they both nod.

Malcolm lifts me bridal style, and my arms slide around his neck. Darcy returns to the end of the tunnel. She glances over her shoulder at us, making sure we're ready to run, then turns back to the wall, cocks her arm back, and slams it into the rock.

At first, I think nothing happened, but then I notice that her arm is embedded up to her elbow. There are cracks in the wall that spider out from her, yet the wall doesn't seem to attack her the way it did me. We all breathe out a sigh of relief.

We're certainly not going to be able to waltz in there just easy as you please, but at least we can take care of the wall that stands between us. We'll need to be careful once we make it into the chamber on the other side. The magic protecting the blade is extremely defensive and volatile. There's really no telling how it's going to react when we get into the chamber, and that makes me nervous as fuck.

DARCY FINISHES BREAKING through the wall. Thankfully, the thing hasn't put up a fuss. It appears that, at least for this part, only magic triggers it to lash out. Malcolm places me on my feet. I'm feeling much better, although my head is still aching. Shifter healing is fast, but it seems a magically induced concussion takes a while to heal. Awesome.

We stand where the wall had once been, leery about stepping into the chamber before us. We don't want to set the magic in here off, so we keep the fireball in the tunnel behind us. It's dark in the chamber, but there's a small platform that seems to be made from hardened magma, and there's a soft glow coming from the top of it. It's a bit too faint to confirm this is where the weapon is, but it's a safe bet to make that assumption. That's where all the magic is concentrated.

"So who wants to be the test dummy?" I'm only half joking. Someone is going to need to try to step up to that platform, and after what happened to me and the wall...I don't want to be it. I instantly put my finger to my nose.

Darcy raises a brow at me and has an expression on her face that tells me she finds my actions juvenile. I don't care. I don't want to get thrown down the tunnel again. She doesn't look as though she's just punched through a rock wall, so she can go.

Malcolm glances between the two of us and lets out a loud, dramatic sigh. "I'll go."

He takes a tentative step into the chamber and his shoulders relax when nothing happens. I let out the breath I hadn't been aware I was holding, but I'm not foolish enough to think he's going to be able to physically grab the weapon without some push back. We just need to determine how to disarm the magical defenses.

I inch my way into the room after Malcolm. The magical signature is oppressive, and it was clearly designed to make anyone who gets near the weapon uncomfortable. Malcolm shifts on his feet like he isn't sure if he should move forward or not. Darcy steps up on my other side. Her face is scrunched as though she's sucking on a lemon. We can all feel it in here.

"While I'm happy we haven't triggered any poison darts or large rolling rocks, I'd really like something to happen so we can figure out what we're dealing with," Malcolm grumbles. He has a point. Springing a booby trap would certainly help us.

"Do you want me to try reaching out with my magic again?" I wince at the wobble in my voice. "I'm willing to take another for the team." I'm really not, but I'm the only one of us who can feel magic this way.

I don't wait for either of them to answer me before reaching out again. The magic pushes back, but it doesn't seem threatened right now since I'm not really invading its space. I'm nudging its outer edges. The sound and feel of this magic has me thinking war drums, a steady pounding rhythm that amps up my adrenaline.

Since it's playing so nice right now, I decide to try a different approach. I keep some magic on the outskirts of the defensive perimeter. At the same time, I start to charge up enough magic to essentially skewer the middle. I'm hoping it'll either give us information on how to get around it, or it'll cleave the protections in half, leaving a small strip for us to get to the sword.

"Get ready," I say as I finish pulling in as much energy as possible to fuel my blast. "I'm not sure how this is going to react."

"It would be great if you didn't get yourself killed, kitten," Malcolm mutters.

"I'm certainly going to try to stay alive, witch." With that, I release my magic.

Chapter Twenty-Two

Several things happen at once.

As though I'm watching all of this in slow motion, I observe as my magic slices cleanly through the magical defenses. At least, it appears to. In the same moment, I feel Ayla's shout down our bond as well as the demons closing in on us.

A shockwave blasts out from my magic's contact with the weapon's defenses. It sends us hurtling either back into the tunnel or into the chamber's walls. Malcolm and Darcy stay in the chamber, but I'm thrust into the tunnel, right at the feet of Malick and a cloaked figure.

I'm envisioning that Lego Batman clip again.

"Malcolm!" My shout rings in my head. I'm not sure if I'm shouting loud enough to get Malcolm's attention or not since my ears are ringing.

Malick and the cloaked being glance down at me. Malick's face is oddly blank. Any time we engaged him in the past, he always had a very expressive face, so to see him like this now is creeping me the fuck out. Big time.

I can't see the face of the person next to him. They are not only covered by a large hooded cloak, they are also using magic to keep their identity secret. I remember Ayla telling me that those who worked with demons felt...fuzzy? Off? And I can feel it now myself. I don't see this person in a blurry way, instead the sound of their magic rings completely off tune.

Scrambling to my feet, I thrust up a magical shield and glance behind me. Darcy is at the mouth of the chamber and Malcolm is just moving into sight. My feet start to slowly inch back toward my friends as my gaze shoots to the wonderful horde of demons currently barring our exit. We already faced the daunting task of trying to figure out a way to get the weapon, now we need to keep it safe and fight our way out.

Once I stand with Darcy and Malcolm, my shield fitted into the opening, I reached out to Ayla through our bond.

Buzz Lightyear to Star Command. Come in, Star Command. Over.

Seriously?

Just making sure you're listening.

There's a whole swarm of demons up here. A few slipped through. Kelly and I can't hold the tunnels open much longer, we need to help Caleb, Dante, and Connor. She sounds frantic and worried.

Malick and a new mage are down here with friends. The weapon is protected by some weird defensive magic. We didn't even get a chance to get close before they came down here.

"Motherforking shirtballs."

I chuckle at her *The Good Place* reference.

Okay... Here's what we'll do. Kelly and I are going to close the tunnel. We'll help take care of the demons topside, then open the tunnel again and send help down. Do you think you can hold them off?

Do we have a choice?

Not really, no.

If you let us die down here, I'm going to haunt your sorry ass for all eternity.

Noted.

The ground rumbles, signaling that we've been cut off from the surface. Now we just need to not die. Totally fine. Just a normal day really.

I had kept the bond open with Darcy and Malcolm so they could hear what was going on without tipping the demons off. Neither of them look too thrilled that we're down here on our own. We're going to need to head back home to the infirmary once this is over.

Casting a quick glance at the weapon, I firm up my stance and brace my shield. Malick and the mage haven't moved yet, but I know they won't stay still forever.

"Malcolm, you need to work on getting that weapon. Darcy and I will hold the demons off." I flick my gaze to his. I can tell he wants to argue, but he nods and inches back toward the platform. "Darcy, I'm going to try to make it so the shield will let you, and only you, come and go. We can pick them off and defend."

Her eyes bleed to black, and she sends me a chilling smile. I'm really glad I'm on the receiving end of her wrath right now. She steps out of the shield and then leans back in. Thankfully, she's able to do both.

"You've been cut off from the surface," the mage remarks. I'm having a hard time determining if the person under the hood is male or female. "Your friends won't be able to stand against the army we brought. Neither can you, for that matter."

Darcy starts laughing. Full-on, psycho belly laughing. Okay. Alright. We have an unhinged vampire, witch, demon hybrid on our hands. Cool. Totally fine.

"Liv," Malcolm calls. "I think I'm going to need you to help me with this."

"Seriously?" I hiss.

"It might take both of us working together to break through," he tries to reason.

"Go," Darcy commands without even a glance over her shoulder.

If we're going to do this, we're going to need to do it fast. Otherwise, Darcy is dead and then we're dead. I inhale deeply and start to pull in as much magic as I can. We're going to need as much firepower as possible.

With a nod, we all move as one. The last thing I see before I focus on Malcolm and the platform are the demons rushing around Malick and the mage as they head for Darcy.

I step over to Malcolm and grab his hand. "Let's do this as fast as possible."

The echoes of the fight start ringing through the chamber, and our leading vampire doesn't seem to be struggling...yet. Malcolm squeezes my hand.

"I need you to funnel your magic into me. I know we haven't worked on this yet, but picture a river as the magic flows its way from you and into me. I'll channel it, give it direction." He sounds far calmer than I feel, but I need to center myself if this is going to work.

I shake out the hand that isn't clasped in Malcolm's before I close my eyes. I focus on the river metaphor Malcolm used, picturing my magic as a flowing stream of amethyst, then I concentrate on our joined hands. The river runs from my center, down my arm, and then from my hand and into Malcolm. I think it's working, because it actually feels as though energy is leaving me and pouring into my mate.

"Good, keep it up, kitten." His voice sounds strained. I don't crack my eyes open out of fear I'll lose my concentration.

I continue to power my magic into Malcolm until there's hardly any left. It feels as though all of the energy has been completely sapped from my body. My legs tremble, and I need to lock my knees to keep me standing upright. Once I've given him all I can, I open my eyes.

Gasping, I try to understand what I'm seeing. Malcolm's face is creased in pain and sweat pours from his forehead. It looks as though he's also having difficulty standing. His entire body is shuddering.

He raises a wobbly hand, his breathing rough and choppy —it's far too labored for my liking. Energy starts to form in his palm. It's a stunning mixture of amethyst and deep forest green. It builds until it's almost the same size as Malcolm.

Just as he's releasing the magic, I hear Darcy scream, "Liv! Watch out!"

Once again, my life moves in slow motion. A sense of dread surges through me as I turn toward Darcy's warning, but it's already too late. Gods. No. My heart slams inside my chest. My lungs freeze.

Someone is screaming. It's a heartbroken sound that, if it continues, will make my ears bleed. My legs give out, and I sink to my knees. My arms fly up.

Malcolm has been skewered with a wicked, black lance. As I watch Malcolm take a single step forward before he sinks to his knees, the magic we made together slams into the platform. That's when I realize I'm the person screaming.

I can still feel Malcolm through our bond, but it's growing weaker. My fury gives me the strength I need to climb to my feet again. It fuels me with more magic and feeds my need for vengeance.

As much as I want to rush to Malcolm's side, I need to destroy the threat. Even if I could heal him, it wouldn't matter if the demons were still around. Darcy is outside the chamber, but Malick and the mage are now in here with us.

We are separated by several feet, but I close the distance in a blink.

Malick still has that odd, blank look on his face. He's not the real threat right now. The mage at his side, however...

That motherfucker is going down.

Chapter Twenty-Three

I summon as much magic as I can into my fist before slamming it into the mage's chest. They stumbled back a few feet, but I don't allow the asshole a moment of respite. I'm right on top of him, raining down strikes without thought.

When the earth starts to shift beneath my feet, causing me to lose my footing, I stop attacking. I quickly glance around. Rocks fall from the ceiling. Shit. The mage is going to bring the entire cave system down on top of us.

Will that set off the volcano? Gods, I hope not.

Before I can reach the mage to stop the cave-in, the roof completely collapses, and when the dust settles, the mage is gone. Fuck.

"Malcolm!" I yell. I'm in a small pocket that barely gives me enough room to stand. "Malcolm, are you alright?" I don't hear anything, so I try our bond. *Malcolm!* He doesn't respond.

My heart beats faster, and I can see my pulse pounding in my eyes. The bond is still there, so he isn't dead.

Darcy, are you okay? I call through the bond.

That depends on your definition of okay.

I sag against the rocks surrounding me when she answers.

The lower half of my body is buried. I'm going to need blood. Preferably now.

I try to calm my breathing and think. Did the mage take the demons? I can't hear anything. I hate not knowing what the hell is going on.

Ayla, I say, reaching out to my friend.

Almost finished up here! She sounds exhausted.

If you could...I don't know...Kill faster, that would be great.

Are you sassing me?

I would never! We're just sort of buried in a cave-in.

What the actual fuck? Lead with that next time. She cuts off the connection.

"Malcolm!" I try again, hoping he was just out cold and maybe awake now, but there's still no response from him.

I tug on my braid, unease spreading through me with skittering legs. I need to get through the rocks without causing further collapse.

Think, Liv. Think!

Inspiration hits. Damn, I'm so happy I'm a nerd.

I inhale deeply through my nose and then exhale slowly through my mouth. I focus some of my magic into my hand, envisioning what I want to create. Ayla has weapons she created out of magic, but this will function as both a tool and a weapon. I take a few more yoga-like breaths before I feel something solidify in my palm.

Looking down, I feel a surge of giddy excitement and a pure, fangirl squee goes through me. I did it! I can't believe I actually did it! *Dios Mio!*

Shining brightly in my right hand is a motherfucking lightsaber. Instead of the canon red, blue, or green, my lightsaber is a shocking pink—and if I'm being real with myself, I'm completely here for it.

Maybe I'm thinking about magic the wrong way. Maybe I should think about it like the Force. A wicked grin spreads across my face. I can totally do this. I slash the lightsaber through the rocks blocking my path to Malcolm, then I extend my hand and focus on pushing the rocks into the chamber while also holding up the roof so I don't cause a larger cave-in.

A few rocks slip my attention, and one beams me right in the nose—which hurts like a bitch—but for the most part, everything does what I need it to. I'm easily able to step into the chamber where Malcolm, Malick, and the weapon are.

Only to find nothing. All three are gone.

My panther screams loudly in my head. Our mate is gone! I frantically search the chamber for some sort of hidden tunnel or way out, but there's nothing.

No. No, no, no.

My hands shake violently, so much so that I have to drop the lightsaber or risk hurting myself.

Take a deep breath, Olivia, my panther, just as anxious and frantic as I am, soothes.

But I can't. I can't just calmly walk out of this godsforsaken hole. I have to find my mate. I need to know what they did to him.

My chest heaves as I struggle to take in air, and spots float in my vision.

My panther surges to the surface, forcing me to shift. That...helps, actually. I'm compelled to take a back seat for a minute, which allows me to slow my spinning mind.

ONCE I'VE GIVEN myself sufficient time to calm down, my panther allows me to retake the reins. Now, I'm standing in the middle of a dormant volcanic chamber naked, but at least I'm calm enough to think of a plan.

They've taken Malcolm. I'm not going to give them the chance to torture him like they tortured Ayla and Darcy. Ayla said when she was held captive, she couldn't reach out to Caleb, and I remember we hadn't been able to reach her either. We'd only been able to firmly lock in on her location after she'd taken down the barrier around her. I'm not sure Malcolm has that sort of time.

The first thing I need to focus on is getting out of this hole with Darcy, so I decide to get to her the same way I got in here, with my handy lightsaber and the Force.

Once I've reached her, I see that getting her out from under the rubble isn't going to be easy. I don't want to wait on the others though. Malcolm had been seriously injured, and if they don't heal him...I don't want to think about that. I also don't want to think about what may happen if they do heal him.

"I'm going to try something," I tell Darcy. "It might not work, and we might both be killed."

"The best kind of plan." Darcy grins up at me, red seeping into her eyes. She'll need a lot of blood to heal.

I allow all of the emotions I pushed back earlier to bubble up to the surface. It feeds my magic until it's a physical force swirling around us. I think about what I want it to do for us, replaying the scene in my head over and over again.

And then I release my hold.

If I thought anything before now had been in slow motion...this is something else. I can see each rock crumble into fine flecks of dust and explode into the air. As I move, everything around me appears to be standing completely still. I crouch and grab Darcy's hand. Then I blink.

We're on the surface.

Time speeds up again, and we both seem to sag to the

ground. Darcy's legs are bleeding heavily. When Dante notices us, he cries out and rushes to her side. The ice is littered with demon bodies, and I can hear the others talking, but I can't make out what they're saying. My gaze in on the hole Darcy and I came out of.

Or, more accurately, the slab of solid ice that doesn't look as though it's ever been disturbed. Did I just...teleport? Is that even a thing?

Large hands lift me up and carry me away from the carnage. My mind keeps racing as I try to piece together what I just did and come to terms with the fact that my mate has been taken by a bunch of demons—that he could be dead.

Gods, please don't let him be dead.

The next time I blink, I'm in the infirmary at the pack-house. I can hear people talking, but all the voices just blur together. My panther is pacing restlessly inside me. Searching...

Mate.

My heart convulses and I cry out.

There are several faces above me, all speaking, all moving. My brain can't seem to make the connections it needs to in order for me to understand what's happening.

The sudden ring of flesh against flesh, followed shortly by a sharp sting on my cheek, has me blinking. My eyes seem to focus, and I'm finally able to start making out what the others are saying.

"Ayla!" Kelly scolds. "She's in shock. You didn't need to slap her."

"We all felt what happened to Malcolm down there. We don't have the luxury of waiting on her to get out of her own head. We need information. Now."

Ayla's right. I need to give them as much information as I can so I can help them save my mate. I take a few deep breaths before sitting up in the bed. A quick glance around tells me that Ayla, Kelly, Connor, and Caleb are currently in the room.

"Darcy is still healing. Dante didn't want to leave her," Kelly whispers, her head bent close to mine.

"We combined our magic to get to the weapon," I start, barely recognizing my own voice, "but somehow that new mage and Malick made it into the chamber. The mage caused the collapse."

"We knew he'd get a new mage." Connor crosses his arms over his chest with a glower. "I'm just surprised he was able to find one so fast."

"He looked weird." The words burst from my lips before I can stop them.

"What do you mean, 'weird?'" Kelly asks.

"His face was blank, like no one was home, and he didn't speak at all. The mage did all the talking for him. He just seemed to be on autopilot." They all look at each other. It's clear none of us know what to make of this information.

"We know from last time that we couldn't sense Ayla, but I highly doubt they'll be able to completely erase the weapon's signature. It was warded to high heaven back in Iceland, and we could still feel it." Connor starts stroking his beard. "The three of you will need to search for it. They were probably able to mute the signature or make it seem like something else. We should have you search known bases and then move out from there. Even if they make it seem like something else, there will still be remnants of that original power, so you'll need to look closely."

"How much will this drain Liv?" Kelly inquires, dragging her gaze over every inch of my body. "Physically she seems fine, but between the shock and energy output she used to get to the surface, she may be running on empty."

"We'll take the load," Ayla offers. "We won't let her take

too much. You and I have enough energy to shoulder the entire search if we need to."

"Guys," I snap. "I'm right fucking here. I'm fine. Let's do this so I can go get my mate and kick everyone's ass."

"Here." Ripley steps forward and thrusts something into my hands. I had no idea the young witch was even here. "Drink this. It'll help with the shock and make sure you're healing any internal injuries."

I nod and down the potion. Gagging, I hand the glass back to her. "What the hell was that?"

"Don't ask." She chuckles. "It should also help boost your magic enough so you won't pass out cold while linked with the others. Just make sure you pace yourself."

"Got it. Thanks."

She scurries off. I'm still surprised with how fast and quiet she is for a witch. I should get Ripley to train some of our combat witches in stealth.

Not now. I force my brain to focus on the task at hand. Tracking down a nearly imperceptible speck of magic in a world full of the stuff should be no problem...right?

Chapter Twenty-Four

When I blink my eyes open, I have a moment of panic, thinking I've gone blind. Everything is just as dark with my eyes open as it was with them closed. I gently rub them and try again. Nothing. Not at first anyway.

A minute goes by. Then another.

A small shaft of light appears on the floor as a door creaks open somewhere above me.

Okay. Not blind. Just in the dark somewhere.

That's when the memories hit. Liv! I surge upright and forward, only to slam into thick, heavy metal bars. I groan and lightly prod my nose. Thankfully it isn't bleeding, so I didn't break it. I run my hands along the cell I'm in. That's exactly what I'm in. A fucking cell.

Liv? Kitten, can you hear me? Silence echoes back.

I take a deep breath in an attempt to force myself to remain calm. What's the last thing I remember?

Getting stabbed in the damn back. My hands fly to my chest and my back, but my wounds have been completely healed. Why the fuck would those assholes heal me? I assume

Malick and his little mage friend took me right after stabbing me, considering I had been the one with my hands around the...weapon.

Fuck!

Where is it? Son of a bitch!

Okay...Okay. So what do I know?

I had been pretty badly wounded right after I touched the weapon. I remember everything around me going black. Now, I am without the weapon and my wounds have been healed, but I can't access my bond with Olivia. I try nudging my bond with Caleb, only to find that one silent as well.

It's like when Ayla went missing. Okay. We were only able to pinpoint her location after she took down a shield.

But—I snap my fingers—if I know Connor as well as I think I do, they won't try to look for *my* magical signature. They'll have already realized I can't be tracked through any of the bonds, which means they'll use something stronger to find me.

I gaze up at the ceiling, despite the fact I can't see it. Assuming those douche canoes—thank you, Ayla, for the colorful cursing—didn't move the weapon to a different location, they'll be trying to track that in the hopes of also finding me. I just need to find a way to confirm the weapon is here and see if I can boost that signal.

The door opens wider, and the sound of slow, steady steps reaches me. Light floods the area, and I curse as I blink the pain from my eyes. Give a guy a warning.

"Witch," Malick hisses as he steps in front of my cell. He doesn't look too hot. His face is far paler than a vampire's, and he has black smudges under his eyes. What the fuck?

"What the hell do you want, demon?" I try to catalog every feature. There's something happening to him, and if it's this drastic, I'm not sure I want to know what it is.

His eyes dart around my cell as though he expects

someone else to be in here with me. That freaks me out enough that I do a quick scan too. There's no one else here, nothing. What the hell is wrong with the archdemon? Malick leans against the cell door, his knuckles white from how hard he's grasping the bars.

"They're going to try to turn you into a sleeper cell," the demon mumbles. I lean in just to make sure I'm hearing him correctly. "I'm going to give you a single window to contact your mate and tell her where you are. One single window. If you miss it, that's on you."

"Why the fuck would you help me?" My eyes narrow on the demon. I don't trust this asshole as far as I can throw him.

A grin spreads across his face. "You can't. I'll admit that much. But I'm only free for short bursts now. I want to take Wrath out just as much as you do. He played me, and I don't like being made into a fool."

My head whips back. Wrath has been controlling him? I try to remember what Ayla told us about her time with Malick. He seemed to be under the impression he would be helping Lucifer, which we now knew wasn't the case.

"Your window will come when the mage leads you upstairs." Malick snaps his fingers in front of my face, drawing my attention back to him. "Do you understand?"

I nod. "Yes. What about you?"

He scoffs. "Don't pretend you care, witch." With that, he's gone.

I SPEND some time pacing my cell before I finally slide to the floor. My mind is still reeling from my encounter with Malick. He's been controlled by Wrath...is *still* being controlled by Wrath. I should start keeping bloody notes.

The door opens again, and a lower-level demon stands in front of my cell. "It's almost time." He unlocks the cell and holds the door open. Standing slowly, I assess the demon's threat level. Do I risk hinging the chance of escape on Malick? Who seems completely unhinged? Or do I attempt to get myself out of this mess? Can I even escape? I'm no queen, and my powers are nonexistent right now.

Bloody cock sucking twat.

My feet seem to move on their own, past the demon, and up the stairs. Looks like I'm winging it then. Right. Once I get to the top of the staircase, the demon scuttles past me, leading me to a plain wooden door. I take in the hall around me. It's stone, possibly limestone based on the color, and old. It's a historic building. Old family home perhaps? Inhaling deeply, I attempt to gather more information.

My sense of smell isn't as strong as a shifter's, but it's better than a human's. I pick up a faint whiff of the ocean as salty, briny air rushes through a window nearby. I also smell the musk of old books coming from the door in front of me —a library or an office perhaps. Unfortunately, however, I don't pick up any scents that give me even the tiniest clue as to where I am.

The demon nudges the door open but doesn't enter the room beyond. Instead, he gestures for me to continue in alone. I lock gazes with the demon, silently telling this asshole he's on my hit list.

"You'll wait in here. Everything is spelled, so don't fucking touch." He shoves me across the threshold and slams the door behind me.

I was right about the room being an office. There's a large fireplace to my left, so huge I could probably stand up in it just fine. There are no logs, and the stone there has been scrubbed until it shines. There's a small window with wooden shutters opposite me, otherwise the wall is blank. A large bookshelf takes up the space to my right. It's filled with old, leather-bound books and parchment scrolls. Too bad everything's been spelled in here. I'd go poking around otherwise.

A massive chandelier hangs above me, emitting just enough light to see. This whole space feels very medieval, which has me rolling my eyes. Of course the bad guy would have a medieval office in a stone fortress of some sort. I sigh internally, how cliché.

I look closer at the bookshelf. Something seems off about it. I step nearer, being careful not to touch it in any way. One panel isn't level with the rest. Odd. Staring, I try to figure out why the hell a single panel, about eye level, wouldn't be even with the rest of the shelves around it. If it were a door, it would make sense if the entire shelf would be off.

"I am well aware of the timeline, Lord Wrath." I freeze. The mage's voice floats into the room. It's so quiet that for a moment, I think I imagined it.

"I don't think you truly are, dear. One of the seals has already been broken." The voice that answers is new. It's masculine, deep, and filled with violence. Isn't Wrath supposed to be sealed in Hell? How the hell is he here with the mage?

"I am aware, my lord. It is easier to contact you with a conduit now. Does this mean your siblings are awake?"

"Indeed. I have not been able to contact them all, but I will. The plan is changing."

"Changing?"

"We still have need of the Fates. Your role has not changed."

"My lord," the mage butts in, "they are searching for the Óirian weapons. They found one right before I intervened. That is why I called you."

There's silence for a moment. That silence is so loaded with the threat of death it has the hairs all over my body standing on end. That mage, and the rest of us, are very lucky Wrath is trapped in Hell.

"Do they have the location of the others?"

Others? Connor said there was only one more. I try to lean closer to the bookshelf to hear better.

"They are aware of one more."

"After you have dealt with their witch, you are to intercept them at all costs, am I understood?"

"Yes, my lord."

"I cannot maintain the tether for much longer. What of Malick?"

"He is...difficult, my lord. He does not wish to be part of our plans, and forcing his compliance with magic takes quite a bit of energy. He fights it."

"Understood. Dispose of him. I have another I can use. I will send you to wake him after you have procured the other weapon."

"Understood, my lord."

I take several careful steps back, but the mage doesn't come from the bookshelf, he comes from the fireplace. He still has the hood covering his face, and based on the conversation I overheard, he's still using magic to hide his voice as well. We study each other for a moment before the mage moves to lean against the desk that takes up the center of the room.

"Malcolm, you have talents you haven't told your friends about." He tsks. "That's not very nice. Keeping secrets from your friends. From your mate."

I stiffen. Before I can respond, I feel a tug against my mate bond.

Kitten! I try to blast as much of my magic down the bond as I can before it's shut down again. Frustrated, I run my hair through my hair and try to think of a way to respond to the mage. This person knows me...knows us. But how?

"I have a special ability just like any other witch." I shrug, playing it off. "All of us have one thing that's unique about us. Mine isn't all that fascinating."

The mage chuckles and shakes his head. "See, that's where I beg to differ." He straightens and moves to circle me. I keep pace so I never give him my back. "Wouldn't you say a witch who can control blood is very fascinating? Especially in a community that includes, say, vampires?"

My fists clench at my sides as I remain silent. I'm not going to give this asshole anything to work off of. Caleb and Connor are the only two who know about that ability. Much like some of the other more "dangerous" bloodlines, my family has been hunted for centuries because of our abilities. We could drain a vampire of all their blood in seconds—or any living thing for that matter. If it has blood, we can use it, and not just to pull it from the body. We make excellent assassins. No one questions a blood clot.

"I plan to use your gift against you. I'm a mimic, you see." Fuck. That's one of the rarest forms of magic. That means this motherfucker can copy any form of magic he comes into contact with. All he would have to do is touch me. Sure, it runs out after a while, but the amount of damage he could do before then is unthinkable.

I start moving in an attempt to keep several feet between us. I need to get out of here. If Olivia didn't hear me, couldn't pinpoint my magic...he can use my blood magic against me. He could spell me to do anything at any time with access to my blood. I have to keep him distracted and pray I can figure something out if Olivia doesn't start attacking soon.

"Mimicry is an extremely rare ability." I keep my voice low and calm. "How have you remained hidden from the Council?"

"The Council is a joke," he spits. "A pathetic attempt to

control the uncontrollable. There are far more of us hidden than those who reside in your ranks."

I have no doubt about that. Ayla alone has proven that to us.

A demon bursts into the door. "Sir, we're under attack."

A wave of rage sweeps through the room before the mage steps toward the door. "Keep him here."

Chapter Twenty-Five

One moment, barely the blink of an eye, was all I got from Malcolm before I couldn't find him again. It felt as though my heart had been ripped from my chest. Gods, this gaping part of me that I had no idea existed until now will eat me alive if I can't get him back.

My panther roars inside me. We *will* get our mate back. We have to.

Thankfully, I was connected to Kelly and Ayla when I felt the blip from Malcolm, and we'd been able to pinpoint a city in Spain. Now that we're here, it's a bit easier to trace the magic of the weapon. There's a lot of old magic here, which isn't surprising, but it's of a different nature than the magic of the weapon.

"There are a shit ton of demons around here," Ayla murmurs as she sidles up next to me. We've been following the impression of the magic in a similar fashion as to what we did in Iceland—which basically means we're aimlessly wandering the streets in a random city in Spain.

Like when we rescued Ayla, we brought quite a bit of backup. No one wanted to sit this one out. Malcolm has wormed his way into the community's heart, and it was actually a struggle to keep people from coming. My heart lurches before plummeting again. I'm not about to assume the worst, but I won't feel right until I'm back with my annoying witch.

We come to a villa that's a few miles from the sea. This is where the pulse is the strongest. I find it interesting that when Ayla had been captured, she'd been taken to a house in the middle of nowhere in Mexico, and now they're in the middle of a damn city. Humans could end up in the crossfire. We'll have to be very careful.

"I can set up a barrier around the villa," Kelly muses as she studies the building. "It should prevent humans from crossing, but it won't help those already inside."

"That's a risk we're going to have to take," Caleb rumbles. "We need to get in there. We can try to get as many humans out as possible, but our main concern is retrieving Malcolm and the weapon with as little damage to the city as possible."

"Understood." Kelly takes a few of the witches we brought with us and starts to erect a barrier, while the rest of us continue to study the villa.

"What's the best way in?" I look over at the others. Dante stayed behind with Darcy, so Xin and a few other vampires came in their place. Connor and Caleb stand behind Ayla and me like gargoyles.

We all move into the courtyard of the villa, the barrier sealing us in. I still can't sense Malcolm, but I'm a little less worried than I was moments before. Caleb shifts and releases a roar that shakes the ground and rattles the windows. It's a battle cry. A call to arms.

Demons start to pour out of the building, all lower-level, and none of them worth my time. Ayla, Kelly, and I make our way calmly past all of the lower-level demons with Connor right behind us. We step into the entryway of the villa and stop. The mage is here, standing mere feet away from me.

There's no sign of Malcolm, and more surprisingly, Malick is missing.

"I'll admit, I thought it would take you much longer to get here. You surprise me."

I hate that we can't identify the mage. Keeping his identity secret like this makes me think we know who this is. Which is worrying.

"Maybe you shouldn't underestimate queens," Ayla retorts. *Go look for Malcolm.*

I give a subtle nod and start to slink away to search for my mate.

More lower-level demons start to move in on them as I slide into the shadows at the edge of the room. It's torture to have to choose between my family and my mate, but we're here to rescue Malcolm, and they'll provide a great distraction until I can find him.

I follow the mage's scent through the hall, quickly realizing that I won't be able to follow my bond to Malcolm, even in here. The scent has a distinct magical smell to it. It's possible the mage is trying to confuse any shifters who try to catalog the scent. They've still got something that blocks it. I can worry about that once I find him.

Before long, I'm standing in front of a plain wooden door. My heart rate picks up and my breath hitches. He's here. I can just feel it. Right behind this door.

As my hand goes to curl around the knob, I hear the sounds of fighting on the other side. Both my panther and I bristle, ready to lay a smackdown on anyone who would put a finger on our mate. I slam the door open and pause at what I see.

Malcolm has a lower-level demon in a headlock, and he's pummeling him with his fist. I try to fight the smirk that wants to curl my lips, but I can't stop the laughter that bubbles up. Malcolm's gaze flies up to meet mine.

"I am here to save the day, fair damsel." I lean against the doorjamb with a brow arched. "Whenever you're ready, lovely maiden."

He pauses his thrashing of the demon to flip me off before he snaps its neck. Crude...but efficient.

"I like your style, my dear." I keep the teasing lilt to my voice to hide the swell of emotion that's rising in my chest at the sight of him. My muscles tremble as I fight the urge to tackle him to the ground. Now isn't the time.

"Kitten, get your perky little ass over here before I have to make it red." Malcolm sighs dramatically and holds out his arms.

I give into the urge and launch myself at him. My arms encircle his neck as my legs wrap around his waist. I bury my nose in the crook of his neck and take deep inhales of his scent. He holds me tightly and squeezes almost to the point of pain.

Malcolm coils my braid around his hand and pulls my head back. We scan each other's face. I don't even realize I'm crying until he wipes a tear away, and my hand automatically lifts to do the same for him. He's crying...about me.

"I love you." I press my lips against his with an urgency that surprises me. The bond bursts to life between us, and I bite back a sob as I continue to kiss my mate.

He pulls me back, resting his forehead against mine. "As much as I'd love to sink my cock into that tight little pussy of yours, we have a demon army to kill. But when this is over, kitten, I'm going to fuck you so hard you won't be able to walk."

"Promise?" I press a light kiss to his lips when he chuckles and releases me.

I take one more moment to just look at him. Healthy. Whole. Mine.

~

WHEN WE MAKE it back to the entryway, it's pure chaos. I can't find Kelly anywhere, Ayla is fighting with her war club, and Connor is in his dire wolf form. Malcolm and I exchange a heated glance before I manifest my lightsaber in my hand, and going for gold, I materialize another one in my other hand. Yeah, baby.

"Okay," Malcolm growls against my ear, "we don't have time now, but the fact that you just created two lightsabers has me so fucking hard it hurts. You're going to choke on my fucking cock as soon as I'm done here. I don't give a fuck if the others watch."

I blush but nod. With a flick of my wrist, I start beheading demons left and right. I can't see the mage anymore, but right now, the focus needs to be on the demons.

A yelp has me spinning to find Connor currently pinned under ten demons, and it looks as though his hind leg is broken. Malcolm and Ayla are fighting to get to him, but more demons just keep pouring into the room. I start slashing my way in that direction, hoping one of us can get to him before it's too late.

A screech has us all—including the demons—whipping our heads up. Another dragon? This one looks different. Instead of four legs, it only has two, and it doesn't shoot fire, it shoots frost. It seems as though it's sucking in a black mass all around it.

"Kelly is a wyvern!" Ayla shouts, glee lacing her tone as she points to the not-dragon above us. "And she's using her sin eating powers!" The maniacal laughter that follows has me quickly wondering who the bad guys are here. That was a seriously evil laugh.

Kelly lands in front of Connor with a thud, her massive

jaws making quick work of the demons attacking him. She then takes up a protective stance above him, lashing out with frost. She doesn't appear to be draining anymore sins.

We finally make it over to them, and Ayla places her hands on Kelly's chest. "You need to change back. If you can drain the demons, we can get out of here faster and get Connor help."

The wyvern snaps at her, snarling low in her throat. Connor returns to his human form, using Malcolm to keep himself upright as he starts to gently run his hands along Kelly's scales.

"It's alright, my little nightmare. I'm safe." Little nightmare? She has been keeping things from us. "Turn back for me."

With a huff, the wyvern leans down and licks Connor before turning into a very naked Kelly. The two stare at each other with such heat, I almost feel the need to look away. It seems as though Connor certainly doesn't have an issue with people looking—Connor is *very* happy to see Kelly—so I firmly glue my eyes onto Malcolm's forehead.

Connor does something completely unexpected. Letting go of Malcolm, he steps into Kelly, fangs bared, and buries them in her neck.

Holy.

Shit.

Kelly's eyes flutter shut for a moment before snapping open, the eyes of the wyvern peering out as she latches onto Connor's neck.

Well...okay then.

They just mate marked each other. Right here. In front of all of us.

Dios mio.

Ayla coughs "I hate to break up the newly mated couple,

but Kelly needs to eat some sins so we can get out of here. Connor, you okay letting her go, big guy?"

A low snarl vibrates from his chest, but he pulls back, keeping Kelly tucked as tightly against him as he can.

"You good, brother?" Malcolm looks him over, more tense than he was when I found him in the office.

"Just get this over with." Connor's voice is tight and laced with his wolf's dominance.

Kelly remains silent and wraps her arms around Connor, resting her head against his chest. She starts to glow. It's soft at first, barely noticeable, but soon she's shining as brightly as the sun. Dark wisps of smoke streak through the air, aiming for Kelly and absorbing into her.

It happens faster than I thought it would, only taking minutes to complete, but soon there are no demons left in the entryway.

"Caleb says the courtyard is clear. Let's get out of here." Ayla turns and heads out.

"What about the mage?" My anger at the mysterious magic user surges back to life.

"He isn't here anymore. We can track him from home. Liv, we need to get our people back so they can heal."

I growl but nod. Ayla is right. Connor needs to have his leg set before it heals in the wrong position, not to mention anyone else who was hurt while we were fighting.

I try to curb my frustration. Malcolm places his arm around my shoulders and kisses the top of my head. That helps center me a bit. At least he's here and he's safe.

"I have a lot to tell everyone once we're all able to sit down together," he says when we're standing in front of a portal to head home. "You aren't going to believe what I learned."

Chapter Twenty-Six

I t takes a few days, but thankfully everyone we brought with us is able to heal. Darcy is back up and on her feet, though Dante is never far from her. Connor has spent the last few days in the infirmary, much to his dismay, and although Kelly has been by his side the entire time, none of the witches have allowed for...conjugal visits.

Our inner circle is now sitting in the dining room for the first time in what feels like a century. Malcolm and I haven't really left my bedroom, and we're planning on heading right back once this meeting is done. I'm sure Kelly and Connor can't wait to be alone either, if the looks he's throwing her way are anything to go on.

Fayden is typing away on her tablet, and she grins at us once we're seated. "While you were all away getting beat up, I took the time to build a war room." Her gaze locks on mine, and I can't stop the smile that spreads across my face. "It has all the same features as the one back in Ireland."

"Bless you, you beautiful creature!" I shove my chair back and race around the table to tackle her with a hug. "You're my favorite sister ever."

Malcolm groans loudly and places his head in his hands. "Don't tell her that. Now she's going to be insufferable." I just stick my tongue out at him in response.

Once I'm seated again, Malcolm begins sharing details about his time in captivity.

"Wait." Connor holds up his hand. "So you're saying the mage can talk to the Sins and there are more than two weapons?"

Malcolm nods. "I have no idea where the others are, or how the mage was able to communicate. He just said he had a conduit."

It's still more for us to go off of than we originally had. The only issue is...

"The mage still has that first weapon, and he was instructed to get the second one before we could get to it." Malcolm places his hands on the table before standing. "But that's not the most interesting thing."

We all go silent, watching him like a hawk. He hasn't told me this part of his little adventure yet.

"It was Malick." We all tense at the archdemon's name. "He's being controlled by the mage. He isn't acting of his own free will."

Ayla snorts back a laugh. "Seriously?"

"I know, I know, but listen." He takes a deep breath, and his eyes meet mine. "When we were in the chamber in Iceland, he had this odd, blank look on his face, right?" I nod. "When I woke up, I was in a cell. He came to see me and he was acting...strange, but his face wasn't blank. He seemed a bit manic, honestly. But it was the conversation between the mage and Wrath that confirmed it for me. They're going to kill him."

"That saves us the trouble." Caleb shrugs. We all nod in agreement. One less enemy we need to worry about.

"No." My gaze flies back to my mate, my brow raised in question. "Just...hear me out."

He pushes away from the table and starts to pace along the side of the room. "If we can get to him first, we can learn everything he knows in exchange for protection."

"Absolutely not!" Ayla and Darcy shout at the same time, slamming their hands on the table.

"I get it. I do. But we won't ever have another chance like this. If we can offer him protection from Wrath and the mage, then we can learn everything he knows. It'll help us in the long run!" Malcolm runs both hands through his hair.

I can only gape at him. Protect an archdemon? Has he gone insane? There's some merit to getting whatever information Malick has to offer, but we should kill him right after he gives it to us. We can't just...keep him. He's not a puppy.

"Why don't we table this discussion for now?" Kelly's voice is soft and soothing. She's always the voice of reason. "I think we're all still a little too raw to have a solid discussion and debate about Malick's potential usefulness. Besides, I doubt the mage will be able to find Malick any time soon. He's spent centuries flying under the radar. We have some time."

Malcolm huffs, folding his arms across his chest, and glowers at us. He's cute when he pouts. I kind of want to pinch his cheeks or smoosh his face between my hands and coo at him. My panther snorts in amusement.

"We can't take too much time," he argues, shooting Kelly a look that says he means business. That causes Connor to growl, his wolf flashing in his eyes. I don't rise to the bait and growl back, but I make it a point to stare at the dire wolf.

"Just a few days," Kelly concedes. "I think we all need a bit of a breather. Besides, we have no way of contacting him."

Malcolm huffs again before finally nodding. Crisis averted.

"Can we get back to other things?" Fayden chimes in. A grin tugs at my lips, and I arch my brow. "Sorry, but we have a lot to handle, and I feel like we're not going to have as much time as we'd like."

"Connor, where is the other weapon? We should focus on the one we know of for now." Kelly turns to smile at her mate. He stares at her with such heat, I start to blush. She ducks her head when he leans in to whisper something in her ear. Whatever it is, she liked it.

"Russia. The other weapon is in Russia." Connor turns back to the table. "Moscow, specifically."

"I think we plan our trip out a bit. See if we can figure out a way to contact Malick before we leave and get everything in order."

We all agree.

~

LATER THAT DAY, Malcolm and I are back in my room. We're going over various ways to attempt to contact Malick. I don't necessarily agree that reaching out to the archdemon is the best idea, but Malcolm believes in it so strongly, I'm willing to roll with it.

"I actually think Ayla, Darcy, or even Kelly may be able to get in touch with him." Malcolm runs his fingers down my spine. I shiver and adjust myself so I'm facing him. "Ayla and Darcy went through that change, so there's a bit of him inside them. They may be able to tap into that. Kelly is a sin eater, so she can probably pinpoint where he is. I'm not too familiar with a sin eater's abilities, but it's worth a shot."

"Let's give Darcy and Kelly a few days before approaching them. We can talk to Ayla right away if you want, but I doubt Darcy will be eager to reach out to Malick after the cave-in, and I know Connor will most likely chew our heads off if we approach Kelly."

"You're right." He grabs my hand and presses a kiss to my palm.

I bask in his touch for a moment, allowing it to settle my panther. "I was so fucking scared." My voice cracks, and I have to swallow before going on. "When I couldn't feel you, I..."

Malcolm sits up and adjusts us so I'm straddling his lap before looping both of his arms around my waist and pressing our foreheads together.

"I know, kitten. I felt the same way. My only thought was getting back to you." The depth of emotion that fills his voice has my heart pounding. "I was going to do whatever it took to get back to you."

"I was ready to level everything and everyone to find you," I admit. "It was so hard focusing past my rage and fear."

Leaning in, Malcolm places a gentle kiss against my lips. I nibble his bottom lip and follow it with a lick to soothe the sting. He tangles his fingers in my hair and angles my head the way he wants, then he pulls back a bit and our gazes lock.

"I remember telling you that you're going to choke on my cock, kitten." I clench my thighs and inhale deeply. "You had to go and create lightsabers, and get me rock fucking hard while we were fighting. I think I also promised to redden your pert little ass."

I try to pull back, but his fist tightens in my hair so I can't move too far away. "You're going to do exactly as I say tonight, kitten." His hand wraps around my throat, and I purr.

With a snap of his fingers, I'm naked. Another snap, and I'm bound to the bed. He positions himself between my legs, hunger illuminating his eyes as he leans down to press a kiss against my inner thigh.

"I thought you wanted me to choke on your cock," I tease.

"After I've tasted you." His dark look causes me to shiver.

Malcolm's lips close around my clit as his fingers slowly sink into my pussy. He sucks hard and scissors his fingers, causing my hips to buck against his mouth. Magical hands start to tease my nipples and hold my hips down. I really need to learn how to do that with my own magic.

The pressure against my clit and the pace of his fingers increase. Soon, I'm moaning his name with each pull of his lips.

Come for me, kitten. Come on my fingers.

My panther purrs at his demand.

I'm so close.

A jolt of magic zings against my clit and my nipples at the same time, and I come with a cry. My legs shake and my head flings back as the orgasm continues to wash through me.

The next thing I know, I'm straddling Malcolm's face with his hands locked on my hips, his magic pushing me down so I can slip his cock between my lips. I lick the head as I wrap one hand around the base and cradle his balls with the other. He groans against my pussy.

I could tease him and make him wait before I slide him deep into my throat, but I can't. I need to work him up so he'll flip me and thrust this thick cock into my pussy. I need him to fuck me raw. I need us to connect and show each other that we're alive and well.

With a deep inhale, I quickly move my lips down his shaft until the head bumps the back of my throat. Malcolm's hips buck against me, and I swallow around him. A soft growl vibrates against my clit. I moan, and he curses softly.

Rather than bobbing my head, I pull his cock out of my mouth just a little before sliding it back down my throat. I focus on swallowing and moaning around him. His pace against my pussy falters. That's the signal I've been waiting for.

I pop my lips off his shaft and give it a loving lick before turning my head to glance back at my mate.

"Please. I need you to fuck me." I keep my voice low and raw.

In a burst of movement, I'm slammed against the wall opposite the bed. My legs wrap around Malcolm's waist as he drives his cock into the hilt. My head falls back against the wall as he pistons in and out of me, his fingers tangling in my hair.

"Look at me, kitten. Watch me as I make you come on my cock."

I blink my eyes open. I hadn't even realized I'd closed them.

"Good girl." Magical hands caress my body, pinch my nipples, and roughly flick my clit.

Our gazes remained locked as whimpers and moans burst from my lips, and groans and snarls slip from his. The slap of flesh against flesh soon drowns out everything else. The feel of him moving inside me is all I know, all I want to ever know from here on out. Just the two of us joined like this.

"Gods, I love your pussy, kitten. It's so damn tight and wet." Malcolm presses a quick kiss to my lips. "I love everything about you, Liv. Everything. I love you more than life itself."

Tears sting the backs of my eyes. "I love you so much."

"Then I need you to come around my cock. I need you to scream my name when you do it."

He sends magic zapping through every sensitive part of my body. My head flings back as I scream his name, my pussy clenching tightly around his cock. I feel him swell right before he comes with a roar.

Panting, I lift my head to once again meet his gaze. "I hope you realize I'm not done with you."

"Oh, kitten. I'm going to have you screaming my name all night. You won't have a voice in the morning." A wicked grin spreads across his face.

"Promises, promises."

Chapter Twenty-Seven

The next morning, a soft knock rouses me from my and Malcolm's tangled heap. Thankfully, he's still sleeping deeply. He hasn't rested much since we brought him home, which has worried me, but it seems multiple rounds of sex wore him out. I reach out to run my fingers through his hair before heading to the door. I'm reluctant to leave him, even for a few minutes.

Cracking the door, I see Kelly standing on the other side. She offers me a soft smile.

"Sorry to wake you," she whispers, "but I wanted to let you and Malcolm know that Connor and I talked about Malcolm's plan to reach out to Malick. We're in."

I blink. "You are?"

She nods. "Yeah. I know Connor was a little heated, but I see the merit in what Malcolm wants to do."

"Not to pry, but have you two...?"

She shakes her head. "Not yet." She blushes. "He was in the infirmary until yesterday. When things got heated last night, I accidentally shifted and couldn't shift back until a little while ago, so we spent the night talking through the bond."

My lips twitch. I don't want to laugh at her, but that's very common for a new shifter. Heightened emotions can cause us to shift unexpectedly.

"I'm sure Connor offered to help you learn to control the shift, but if you want someone else to work with, let me know."

"Thanks." She laughs. "It's certainly awkward suddenly shifting into a wyvern when you're turned on. We were both pretty surprised."

"It's typical, but you'll get a handle on it. I don't know anyone who's as on top of things as you are." I pull her in for a hug.

"I'm going to get to work trying to locate Malick. I'll let everyone one know once I have something. I can't promise anything, and I may need a magical boost. I'm still learning how to use my other powers."

"Hey." I hold my hand up. "All that matters is that you're trying. Thank you."

≈

A FEW DAYS LATER, Kelly and I are outside, practicing controlling her shifting abilities. She's getting a lot better, but she still shifts whenever she gets turned on, which has her a little cranky. Not that I blame her. If I couldn't have sex with Malcolm because I couldn't control my shifting, I'd be pissed as hell too.

"I think I can make contact," she says as she lies on the grass, panting. "With Malick. I think I found him."

I bolt to my feet. "What? When did this happen?"

"Last night." Kelly sits up and tilts her head to study me.

"If we're going to do this it needs to be all hands on deck. Darcy is the only one still against this."

I nod absentmindedly. Malcolm, Connor, Kelly, and I talked to everyone the last few days in an attempt to get everyone on board with Malcolm's plan. Darcy is still very much against reaching out to the archdemon.

I understand her reasoning, but the enemy of my enemy and all that. He has information we can use. We don't need to keep him alive after we get it.

"Do what you need to do to get ready. I'll go get Ayla, and we'll talk to Darcy."

"Liv..." Kelly's soft tone stops me from rushing away. "Don't push her too much. We can't lose her."

"I know." I sigh and tug on my braid. "I won't go balls to the wall, and I'll help tone Ayla down."

Kelly snorts a laugh. "Good luck with that."

Yeah, trying to contain our best friend is like trying to trap a tornado. You don't.

Once I track Ayla down, we head off in search of our newest bestie. There are only a few places she haunts so it shouldn't be too hard to find her.

"You're sure you're on board with this?" I ask Ayla. "You're not just doing this to shut me up, right?"

She throws me a look that screams I should shut up right now and rolls her eyes. "Do I do things like this if I don't want to?"

"No."

"There you go." Valid point.

"How are you feeling?" I gesture to her abdomen.

"All I want to do is eat and sleep. I dream about food, Liv."

I laugh, not in the least surprised by this admission.

"But I feel fine. Healthy. Stronger. Caleb says I'm moody

—whatever the fuck that means." She huffs and crosses her arms.

I have to fight the laugh that wants to bubble up. "Men are so stupid." She shoots me another look because I can't quite keep the laughter from my voice.

We finally track Darcy down in the gym. She's been coming here a lot since her injury. I think it has something to do with the feeling of helplessness. She was powerless when she was with Malick, and then again during the cave-in. She doesn't want to feel like that again. Not that I can blame her.

"Hey," I say as I take a seat on the floor against the wall.

"I know why you're both here." Darcy sounds pissed, so this is going to go really well. "Fine. Do it."

Well...that wasn't what I was expecting.

"Darcy," Ayla murmurs.

"No. Look, it's fine. Dante, Xin, and I talked it over. Malcolm is right. You're all right. There's more to gain here than there is risk. Especially after what Malcolm overheard." Darcy massages her temples as she turns to look at us. "It doesn't sit right, and probably won't ever sit right, but I shouldn't be the block here."

She lowers herself in front of us and starts to stretch out. "Just...promise me we'll have every protection we can think of."

I nod. That's fair.

"Absolutely," Ayla assures her. "We aren't going to go into this half-cocked, and I'll even let you be the one to kill him."

Darcy grins. "As much as I'd love that, killing him would require my queen powers to come in, and I'm not sure I want to wait that long for that asshole to die."

"Valid point. I'll let you tell *me* how to kill him." Ayla smiles at Darcy, who nods in agreement.

"Deal."

"Okay." I stand. "Let's go contact a demon." Five words I never thought I would ever utter in my life.

Epilogue

MALICK

I've been on the run for a few days now. Once I'd given that window to the witch, I couldn't stay. I knew I'd served my usefulness, just as I knew I'd been very thoroughly used. The thought still enrages me.

Yet I can't seem to pull myself away from this mess entirely. I still feel the need to continue the search for Ayla's sisters. I glance down at the weapon in my hand. This sword can kill Wrath. If that piece of shit ever gets out of Hell, this can kill him. I can kill him.

I've been starting to think that maybe it's time I take my destiny into my own hands. My purpose in this realm is to cause chaos, so what better way to do that than to be completely unpredictable? To side with those no one thinks I'd ever reach out to? Chaos, by its very definition, is disorder and confusion. Teaming up with the queens would certainly cause that in spades. So would killing Wrath.

I've had to mute my magical signature to make it harder for Wrath's newest puppet to find me. I'm still trying to figure out who, exactly, the mage is. I'm also still trying to determine exactly how much of my past is truly my own versus what was done because of Wrath.

It's...irritating not knowing who you are after a millennium of certainty, but there's nothing I can do about that now other than slowly unravel my actions.

There's a soft knock in my head. I've apparently finally gone completely insane. Groaning, I attempt to ignore the sound, but it only gets louder and more insistent.

"What?" Hadn't meant to actually yell that aloud.

"Hello, Malick."

I still. "Little qu—I mean, Ayla?" Why on earth would she be contacting me?

"I'm going to make this quick. I've got an offer for you."

"Do go on. I'm all ears." I feel an odd sort of exhilaration flow through me.

"We want whatever information you have on Wrath. In exchange, we're willing to offer protection from him."

"How very generous of you, but I noticed that you said just from him. Am I to assume I am not safe from you?"

"We...haven't decided what to do with you after you've given us the information." At least she doesn't embarrass herself by lying.

"I'll think about it." I slam the connection shut. It seems I have more to think about, more destiny to grab on to.

~

Wrath

I NEED TO KILL SOMETHING, strangle something with my bare hands, then bathe in blood. The rage inside me is reaching unmanageable levels.

When I get out of this fucking pit, I am going to raze every single fucking thing and then light it on fire.

I will teach all those who think to stand against me who I truly am.

About Beth

Beth is a loving wife and mother--both of the human and fur variety--best friend, enemy, *that* coworker, work wife, hero, and all around sarcastic badass. She advocates to get rid of the stigma around mental health--having CPTSD, anxiety, depression, and panic. She advocates for the understanding of ADHD in girls and women, having ADHD herself, and she wasn't diagnosed until she was thirty. When she isn't writing, she's playing with her young son, getting sassy with her husband, reading with the cats, roughhousing with the doggo, or sleeping for days. She loves to hear from fans and makes an effort to answer any messages sent her way and like any posts she's tagged in.

Make sure to follow me on social media!

• Instagram: @authorelizabethbrown

• Twitter: @authorelizabet3

• TikTok: RomanceAuthorBethBrown

• Facebook Group: Beth's Resurrected Queens

• Subscribe to my website: authorelizabethbrown.com (I blog, provide a twice weekly newsletter, and post **extras** from all my series!)

- Feel free to shoot me an email: authorelizabethbrown@gmail.com

Also by Elizabeth Brown

The Resurrection of Queens Series

Discovery of a Queen (The Resurrection of Queens, Book 1)—Now available on all platforms!

Vengeance of a Queen (The Resurrection of Queens, Book 2)—Now available on all platforms!

Freedom's Harem Series (Elizabeth Brown & Torri Heat)

Blood Crown—Available on all platforms now!

Made in the USA
Middletown, DE
05 September 2021

46844774R00146